heaven's sweet embrace

Library of Congress Cataloging-in-Publication Data

Kramer, Sheri
Heaven's Sweet Embrace/Sheri Kramer
p. cm.
ISBN 978-1-948796-20-0
Library of Congress Control Number: 2018945014

Book and cover design by Doug Munson
Photo by Sheri Kramer

This is a work of fiction. Names, characters, places, and incidents—
other than those recorded by historians and biographers—are the
product of the author's imagination or are used fictionally. Any
resemblance to any events or persons, living or dead, is purely
coincidental.

Bulk purchase discounts, for educational purposes, are available.
Contact the publisher for more information.

First Printing, 2018

Epigraph Books
22 East Market Street, Suite 304
Rhinebeck, NY 12572
www.sherikramer.com

heaven's sweet embrace

SHERI KRAMER

Epigraph Books
Rhinebeck, New York

PROLOGUE

In the blink of an eye time can collapse and the curtain between lives blow open before settling back in place. I'm sure it happens all the time, ignored, unnoticed. Go ahead. Close your eyes and imagine such a moment. Who are you? Where are you? Imagine your many selves in that moment all aware of you, as you are of them.

Now who are you? Are you still a single self trapped in the confines of time? Let's assume you're not. What tale would you weave of the variation on a theme called your lives here on Earth? To what end are you here?

There, I see it now, the dawning, the light in your eyes. Yes, it's true, you, in all your myriad forms, are on a hero's journey. Wandering through time and space, stumbling, tripping, running, crawling, dancing toward wisdom, compassion, and, most importantly, love.

Look around—family, your friends, even your enemies, they're all on the same journey, the warp to your weft. The anchor points in your eternity.

Believe it or not, you are the director, co-writer, and lead actor on these stages, in these pages. What journey would you take us on? Would you like me to share a bit of mine? Where should I begin when there is no beginning? What ending when there is no end?

I'll start with the man at the tavern.

KORYO 1

(13th century Korea)

There he sits at the tavern; comfortable with his companions, sitting together on one of several platforms, the low table before him covered with bowls of rice wine, greasy chicken, tasty side dishes. Dressed in his rough hemp peasant pants and jacket, his short black beard stands out. Stocky, sturdy, he also wears an air of confidence. Today he is celebrating. And why not? It's a beautiful spring day, the sky is deep blue and the chill of winter has been swept away. He and his companions are filled with hope. Discord in the land has finally given him the opportunity to set himself free.

The years of working the land only to give most or all of the crops away in taxes and levees are finally over. The arrogance, greed, and ineptitude of the ruling class gave him no reason to continue in virtual servitude to ungrateful overlords who only wanted more. He knew he was more than a farm animal even if they didn't. He had paid for his freedom with the lives of his parents and siblings—worked to death or taken into slavery when taxes couldn't be paid. But this is not a time for bitter thoughts. This is a time for rejoicing, even if only for a moment before the next reality sets in.

And so he and his two companions, having met as they traveled into town, drink and sing and eat their fill. They talk of their dreams and scarcely thought out plans. And at the end of the evening stumble into the woods to find shelter for the night.

Shin Seo feels at home amongst the trees. He had learned to hunt small game as a young boy since there was rarely enough to eat, becoming proficient with a slingshot. In his years of conscripted service, he also learned well how to use a bow and arrow, and how to wield a knife. He was strong and quick and possessed the stealth of a hunter.

It was a clear night. The stars were bright and plentiful through the canopy of trees. While beautiful, it meant it would be a cold night. He and his companions needed to find shelter so they headed up the mountainside to find a cave, gathering firewood along the way.

When they find one, it isn't empty. There's already a family inside. Huddled and frightened, runaway slaves. The man holds his wife who is cradling their infant child. A young girl, curled up tight, rests her head in his lap, her small hands holding onto her mother's long skirt, an almost imperceptible smile on her lips as she sleeps, dreams of other worlds.

The cave is large enough to accommodate them all. Shin Seo and his friends quickly build a fire and set out what bedding they have. All are tired. The complications and plans will be sorted out in the morning. His belly full, sleep comes quickly.

UKRAINE 1

Finally, it's dark. Oddly it's the dark that wakes Rivka up now, the setting of the sun means it's time to continue their journey.

Rivka silently takes Hannah by the hand and leads her out of the barn and into the night. Hannah is still half asleep but the chill of the night wakes her. Her feet are blistered and sore as are Rivka's. Rivka silently curses the Russians who won't let her leave like a human being. She and her daughter have been turned into some kind of nocturnal creatures skulking in the shadows, avoiding humans.

It wasn't supposed to be like this.

When her husband left eight years ago he was supposed to send for her as soon as he got settled. She couldn't decide who was worse, the Tsar or the Communists. She spat on them all.

They were heading west with no more than the stars and her instinct to survive to guide her; though, at times, she couldn't help but feel that she had been through this before. Somehow, she knew how to keep them going through the fields and the woods, even though she'd never ventured far from her shtetl before.

Hannah's crying brought her back to the present. Stop crying, someone will hear you! Stop crying.

Koryo 1a

Shin Seo wakes, heart pounding, to the baby crying —haunting impression of a dream in an unknown land lingering, a woman and her daughter.

As the mother gives her breast to the hungry infant, Shin Seo tries to capture his dream, but it's too strange. He knows the people in the dream are frightened, on a dangerous journey, but that is all he can conjure before the dream fades, receding like the ocean as the tide goes out, leaving traces, clues, nothing more as he drifts back to sleep, back to his dream.

Ukraine 1a

Hannah had stumbled and skinned her knee. Rivka cradles her, rocks her, as much to muffle her cries as to comfort. It's too dark to see how badly Hannah is hurt. Rivka strokes her, caresses the hair out of Hannah's eyes, kisses her forehead, then sets her on her feet again. Reminded that she has to stay focused, Rivka checks the sky on this moonless night to get her bearings and heads west. How many days has it been since they began their journey? A week? A month? It's best not to think about time passing, better to draw on whatever good exists in each moment—the warm night breeze, the smell of the earth after the rain, the curve of her daughter's spine against her belly.

Rivka's gift is a natural love of life. Without it she wouldn't have come so far on this trek where every step brings her that much closer to freedom. She gently urges Hannah to her feet and, hand-in-hand, they set off in silence acutely aware of the night sounds around them. Some nights Rivka could swear she hears the blossoms budding on the trees.

Hannah too listens intently to the symphony of crickets, cicadas, and frogs. She sees them in her mind's eye busy finding each other. In a way, it's no different than she and her mother busy finding her father, only, if they are to reach him, they must stay quiet and invisible.

Hannah has only ever seen her father in a picture. She can barely imagine what it will be like to have a father. Will he hug and kiss her with abandon the way her mother does? What if he doesn't like her.

Rivka has similar thoughts about the husband she barely knows. She met him at the wedding and a year later he was gone. He wasn't an affectionate man, though he didn't lack in passion and appreciation of her beauty. Would he still find her desirable?

She had heard stories of America and wasn't sorry to leave this life behind. It was hard to fathom being amongst all those people living together in one place. The thought of electric lights and running water brought a smile to her lips as the mother and daughter plodded on, one foot in front of the other, keeping the North Star to their right.

Another night lost in thought until the time comes to find a safe place to hide and sleep the day away like bats.

KORYO 2

As he is waking, traces of his dream remain, strange. He was a woman in a place unfamiliar to him. It was night and he as she, was running away; walking through fields with a young daughter.

He opened his eyes to see the young girl, sitting on her haunches, staring at him. A chill went through him; she seemed so familiar and she was looking at him as if she knew him, but that was impossible.

She moved towards him, sat, and put her hand on his face, smoothed his hair as she continued to look at him. It seemed so natural, and at the same time equally disconcerting. The spell was broken when she heard her mother stir and ran back to her.

Once everyone was awake, Shin Seo's companions were itching to move on, possibly to join one of the gangs of peasants preying on the elite. Shin Seo wasn't interested in a bandit's life, and so they decided to part ways—that, for the time being, he and the family would stay together.

Shin Seo learned that the family had been the slaves of an official in the countryside. The master had no qualms about taking whichever women of the household he wanted. Chang Mi's baby brother was proof of that; he was conceived while her father was on corvee duty. But he was especially fond of young girls. And so Chang Mi's parents decided it was better to face the risks of running away than of having her raped by the master. They had been traveling a grueling eight to ten hours a day for two weeks, reaching the cave not long before Shin Seo. Though they felt confident that they were well away from their master's estate, they knew they were still far from being safe.

The father knew how to wield a weapon. He had also taught himself how to read a little. The mother was adept at sewing and cooking; skills she had been teaching her daughter. Chang Mi knew how to be quiet and stay out of people's way when the occasion demanded it, but was generally cheerful and curious. And when she smiled, well, everything felt lighter, brighter.

They were relatively unconcerned about food. Shin Seo had some money for rice and other staples and the mountainside was well-stocked with food to hunt or harvest.

The main problem was the bandits and soldiers looking for each other and anyone else who might be of interest to them. So the cave was only a temporary solution until they could come up with a more permanent plan.

Once Shin Seo's companions had left, he and the family sat together eating the rice porridge the mother had prepared. They spoke very little, each of them wrapped in his own thoughts.

Shin Seo heard Chang Mi's mother quietly scold her to leave him alone, to stop staring at him, to come sit with her. But Chang Mi was glued to his side whether he acknowledged her presence or not. For a moment, he looked into her eyes and quickly turned back to his breakfast, unnerved. He finished up and excused himself to go wander the hillside, hoping perhaps a plan would make itself known.

He made his way down to the town to see what gossip might be heard in the market. Strolling through the market stalls, he kept finding things that he thought Chang Mi might like. He resisted until he found a small hair ornament reminiscent of one his mother used to wear. For some reason, he broke down and bought it for her.

It gave him an odd delight to know he had a gift for her stashed in his jacket. He smiled as he imagined the look on her face when he gave it to her. A shiver ran through him as goosebumps rippled his forearms. He quickly shifted his thoughts to lunch.

Back at the tavern, he found a table near a group of nobles, yangban, so he could unobtrusively listen to their conversation. As he slowly ate his meal he listened to them comparing adventures at the kisaing house. He couldn't help but wonder where his sister might be. Is she a concubine or was she perhaps one of the women being discussed by these yangban. Or did she end up a kitchen slave. He suppressed the desire to see her knowing that nothing good would come of it. Even so, the unwanted image of her being taken away as a young girl in lieu of an unpayable grain tax in a year of drought played itself out in his mind's eye.

The memory lingered as he listened to the yangban

talk about the lowborns, the peasants, slaves, and crafts-men—the people without whom they wouldn't be able to survive—as if they were less than human. It was clear the yangban thought the lowborns' only reason to exist was to serve them.

Despite the roiling rage, he sat quietly, slowly eating his meal, hoping to hear something that could be useful to him as he planned his and the family's future. They talked about various skirmishes between the peasants and the landlords, and the increasing number of fields lying fallow.

There was one young man who stayed silent during their banter. He was dressed like them, born into their world, but was not one of them. Shin Seo could see this yangban had a depth to him that could someday put him in danger, that he was someone who had his own thoughts and opinions.

Unlike the others, the young man noticed Shin Seo, knew he was listening to their every word, and almost imperceptibly nodded towards him. Oddly, they both knew that they had more in common with each other than the man did with his peers.

The yangban got up to leave, Han Jin taking just a bit longer than the rest. As he passed Shin Seo's table, he dropped a scrap of paper and walked on. Shin Seo picked it up and put it in his jacket to decipher later.

He took his time walking back to the cave. After all the years of virtual slavery, he savored every moment of freedom. Not wanting to be followed, he picked his way carefully, quietly, focusing all his senses on his surroundings. Fortunately it was another beautiful day. The trees were just beginning to blossom, the bees emerging from their hives, lured by the sweet scent of nectar.

He arrived at the cave late in the afternoon. The family was relieved to see him. They thought perhaps he had thought better of his decision to stay with them. They didn't know to trust him yet. He was greeted with Chang Mi's beaming smile. She had just lost a front tooth. A perfect excuse for him to have a treat for her. He slowly pulled out the gift, tied up in paper, and handed it to her. Smiling from ear to ear, unable to hide her excitement, she unwrapped it as fast as her small hands could manage. But when she pulled the ornament out of the paper, tears welled up in her eyes. He thought perhaps he had done something wrong until she wrapped her little arms around his waist before running over to her mother showing off her new treasure and begging her to put it in her hair.

After fixing the ornament in Chang Mi's hair, the mother looked up with gratitude. Who was this man her daughter was already so attached to, this man of inexplicable generosity?

Shin Seo and the father went out to forage for dinner. Shin Seo had always loved wandering through in the woods, loved to listen to the music of the birds. He looked up to see one carefully weaving twigs, building a nest to house its soon-to-be young. An image of the girl, Chang Mi, stroking his hair came to him; it reminded him of how his mother used to do the same thing. He closed his eyes and indulged in the memory, his head on her lap as she quietly sang him to sleep. Where was she now? Heaven? Reborn into a better life? He missed her love, her laugh, her voice.

The father came up beside him, startling him back to the moment. He's holding a hare up by the ears, lifeless, bloodstained. They forage for some mushrooms, mandrake, and greens and head back silently. When they get back to the cave, the fire is ready to roast the hare. Shin Seo heads back out to get some water from the stream that cuts through the hillside.

The beauty around him is astounding, almost blocking out any concern he has for the uncertain direction his life is taking. On the face of it, staying with this family seems risky, lacking the flexibility he would have on his own. But something inside him says this is the correct path.

Chang Mi sits next to him during their meal, carefully laying tasty bits of rabbit on his rice. Shin Seo is still unnerved by her familiarity. Each time she puts on a morsel, she looks up and smiles. She can't be more than six or seven years old, but her eyes hold the depth of someone much older. She knows exactly which pieces are his favorites and seems to delight in supplying them. He finds it hard to focus on the conversation the father has begun with him.

The father thinks it would be best for them to head north towards the border; beyond the hands of the soldiers. Shin Seo isn't sure. With so many fleeing Koryo, would they just end up as slaves in a foreign land? One thing he is sure of, he didn't leave the life of a peasant to become a slave. It was freedom that he desired. As long as he is free he'll find a way to support himself.

Nothing could be agreed on. It was too soon, it was best to consider their options carefully. So off to bed they went, each trying to imagine a future, unimaginable in its possibilities.

MONGOLIA 1

Galloping at full speed against the biting wind, he wheels around pulling an arrow from his quiver. Thwack. Disappointment. Once again he's wide of the target. Again. The rush of the wind on his face, one with his horse as they turn and shoot. Better. He won't go back to the camp until he hits his target consistently. So far, he's hit it twice, but it's still a struggle and he refuses to be humiliated again.

He's small for his age, but is a better rider than any of his peers. He was practically born on a horse, his mother dismounting just in time to squat and let him out. Within hours he was back on a horse, strapped to her back as they continued the journey to their next encampment.

He preferred spears to arrows, they offered a shorter range, but there was something in their heft, in the throw that made his heart race. And you could take down a doe with a good throw. But no one cared about his preferences. If he couldn't shoot arrows with speed and accuracy, he couldn't fight with the troops.

Again and again, he rode and shot until his thumb was blistered and bloody and he'd hit his target nine times out of ten. Only then did he think to take a rest.

Looking up at the sound of hooves, he sees his brother riding toward him. For the first time he notices the reds of the setting sun. He charges toward his brother who turns and races him back to the camp.

Only two years apart, the competition between them is fierce. As they race each can sense the other's location without having to look. All they can hear is the sound of hooves pounding the dirt and the wind—the wind, almost wet with the coming storm. His brother may be the better archer, but no one anywhere near his age can outride Mongke. His heart skips a beat as he passes his brother, the gap widening just enough for there to be a clear victor when they reach the edge of the encampment.

As they walk past yurts and cooking fires, their stomachs, answering the call of the aromas carried by the smoke, suddenly feel empty. All they can think about is getting home so they can eat.

Their sisters, busy preparing the evening meal, barely take notice of the boys as they approach. Their parents seem to be arguing about something, each is firmly rooted to their point of view. When they finally notice the boys, they break off and move into the yurt, seating themselves on the thick carpet for the evening meal.

Mongke desperately wants to boast about the afternoon's achievement, but doesn't dare break the heavy silence his parents have brought to the circle. Finally, his father asks where he's been all afternoon and his pride in his achievement pours out in a burst of excitement.

His father looks at him intently. "Tomorrow you'll be

tested." From the way his mother is glaring at his father, it's now clear why they were arguing. She's already lost one child and doesn't seem able to bring any more into the world. Even so, he can't hide his excitement. If he passes, if he can prove his skill, he'll be able to join the troops in battle, he'll be a man. He's already spent a year helping with supplies and horses. If they only let him join them, he knows he can prove his worth.

He doesn't hear any of the conversation during the meal and barely tastes his food. Instead, he's going through the all the skills he'll be tested on. Imagining the feel of the horse at gallop, pulling back the bow, aiming, and perfectly hitting the target. Imagining putting his horse through the paces of the course, he and his horse as one.

He's pulled back to the meal after his mother calls his name for the fourth time, his brother's elbow digging into his ribs. It takes him a moment to fully comprehend where he is. His mother is still angry, trying to convince him to wait another year. He looks over at his father who, having said his piece, will say no more. It's up to Mongke to stand up to his mother himself.

As the youngest child, he and his mother have a special bond. He wishes he could tell her he'll wait, but he's already in his twelfth year and anxious to prove himself as a Mongolian man. Rather than try to argue with her, he takes a choice piece of meat from his bowl and places it in hers. At this gesture, tears well up in her eyes. She's been defeated. She knows nothing she can say will deter him. She can only hope he doesn't pass the testing.

The rest of the meal is quiet out of respect for her sorrow.

When his father rises from the table to signal the end of the meal, Mongke goes outside to clear his head. The wind is still fierce, the stars obliterated by the heavy clouds. Lightening pierces the sky and the heavens rumble in response. Finally, the clouds let loose their load and the rain comes pouring down. He waits until he's completely soaked before going back inside. He changes his tunic and pants and hangs the wet clothes by the fire to dry before laying down next to his brother.

He imagines the thunder is the pounding hooves of the army charging its prey as he drifts into sleep.

KORYO 3

Morning. Shin Seo awakes to the smell of porridge. Chang Mi breaks into a smile when she sees his eyes open. Apparently she's been waiting for this moment for quite awhile. She urges him to get up quickly and wash so they can eat. He's still groggy. A vague weariness, his feet aching slightly, as the fog of sleep fades. As he stands up, Chang Mi quickly comes to fold his bedding for him and put it away. An inexplicable wave of affection for this child comes over him, his eyes tearing up at the depth of it.

At that moment, Chang Mi looks up at him, pressing his hand to her cheek. She can't believe it's him. The gratitude she feels at being reunited with her son is beyond words. Especially since he clearly doesn't know who she is. How could he know that it was she who rocked him to sleep every night when he was a boy. That it was she who lovingly cooked his meals and found such joy watching him grow. Would he ever know? What a gift to be able to see what a fine young man he had become.

Shin Seo pulls away, worried at what her mother will think. He walks out of the cave into the fresh new day. It rained during the night. He closes his eyes as he breathes in the smell of spring. When he opens them, the colors are vibrating in their vividness. He marvels at the beauty surrounding him, at his happiness. He thinks of his mother who taught him to appreciate and know the life around him. It strikes him as odd that his thoughts keep turning to her. Perhaps it's only natural now that he is being reborn into a new life.

He wends his way to the stream where he bathes in the cold mountain water. Fully submerged, fully alive, free. He emerges from the water, skin tingling. A ray of sunshine breaks through a cloud, and he feels its warmth. Life is filled with contrasts, each with its own nuanced beauty, each its own perils. He mustn't get complacent in his joy for in these times it can be so easily taken away. He walks back slowly, enjoying the contrast of the cool morning air and the warm sun on his face.

Back at the cave, he joins the family for breakfast. Chang Mi sits between her parents. They sacrificed everything for her. Little do they know that in doing so they've given her the most amazing gift. Her heart is ready to burst with the overwhelming love she feels for these three.

Shin Seo remembers that the father knows how to read. He pulls out the paper the yangban at the tavern gave him and hands it to the father asking if he can understand what it says. Tae Moon carefully unfolds it, looks up, and asks where he got it. Shin Seo recounts the meeting at the tavern. Tae Moon returns his attention to the paper. It has the name of a bookseller's stall and a time, dusk. Nothing more. They look at each other. Dare he meet this young noble? What could he possibly want?

They continue to eat in silence, everyone trying to

imagine the unimaginable; their future. Still, it's too soon to talk about it, too may unknowns, and Shin Seo is the only one with the freedom to wander, to gather information so the picture can be filled in.

When they're done with breakfast Chang Mi helps her mother clean up and then begs Shin Seo to play with her. She's gathered the perfect stones. Throw all but one in front of you, then toss the one in the air and gather the others up before catching the one in the air. She, with her nimble fingers, is much better at it than he. But it's a fun challenge and an excuse to be together. Shin Seo has begun to give in to his urge to spend time with this girl who looks at him as if she's always known him. After losing several rounds of this game she calls gong, he stands up, preparing to set off to get a better sense of the area around the cave before heading into the town.

A sharp wind is blowing, the sky overcast. It was on just such a day that his mother lay dying, too weak to eat the porridge his sister had made. Even so, she tried to comfort him as the tears streamed down his face. Though she couldn't say anything, she smiled at him, looked at him with so much love. Perhaps she was pleased to be leaving such a difficult life. Perhaps she trusted him to find his way without her. All he knows is that she closed her eyes and let out her last breath with the smile still on her lips.

When his thoughts return to the present, he's still standing just a few yards from the mouth of the cave where Chang Mi is waiting for him to notice her, a smile on her upturned face. A chill runs through him as he turns away from her gaze, tears in his eyes. She places a smooth stone in his hand. She'd picked it out just for him, something to keep with him as he wanders around. He drops on his haunches, burying his head in his arms, the tears flowing, grief mixed with joy.

He'd forgotten what it felt like to be loved.

When he looked up, she was gone. He stood up, took a deep breath, and walked out into the hillside. As he walked, he rubbed the stone in his hand with his thumb, felt its smoothness. It was somehow soothing. And when he had finally shaken off all the myriad emotions of the morning, he carefully placed it inside his jacket next to the folded up piece of paper.

He decides to go further up the hillside, carefully noting the trails, the different types of trees, the vegetation, and the various creatures that skitter away at his approach. About half way up to the crest, he hears voices and hides behind a large tree. It seems to be four private soldiers dragging off a run-away slave, his hands bound to his waist, his clothes torn and bloodied. Shin Seo makes sure to stay hidden, noting the scorn the soldiers have for the slave. It is still beyond his comprehension, this world he lives in where human beings are treated like livestock.

When they were out of site, he resumed his wandering. The encounter cementing his resolve to protect this family. To do so, he'll have to learn every inch of their surroundings, every escape route, every hiding place. After a few hours learning the hillside, he ventured back to town for a meal before finding the bookseller's stall.

He ate quickly, absorbed in his thoughts and imaginings, barely tasting his meal. Then he pulled out the piece of paper and studied the characters, memorizing them so he could find the stall without drawing attention to himself. It was still early. He had plenty of time before dusk. He wandered through the market, always amazed at the variety of goods, stopping here and there. He even stopped to buy more rice and some vegetables.

He found one stall filled with books and writing supplies, but the characters on the banner over the shop didn't match the ones on the paper. Finally, he found it. The young noble was already there, perusing a book. Shin Seo isn't quite sure what to do. He's relieved when the yangban looks up from his book and nods slightly. Without uttering a word, he puts the book down and walks out of the stall. Shin Seo follows him, a few paces behind. After walking a circuitous path, the yangban finally turns down a small street and into a shed. Shin Seo follows him in.

The room is empty save for some crates stacked up against the far wall and a straw mat in the center with a couple of empty crates to sit on. The yangban invites Shin Seo to sit. He appears to be a couple of years younger than Shin Seo, but it's hard to tell given the difference in how they've lived their lives.

Shin Seo waits silently, eyes downcast, for the yangban to speak. Finally he begins. Han Jin explains that he is disturbed at the way the ruling classes wield their power. He doesn't know how or if he can actually change anything, but he is determined to do something, to be different from them. Shin Seo listened, unsure what to make of it. He needs help, but can he trust this stranger. What are this stranger's true intentions.

Unprompted, Han Jin tells Shin Seo that his father is a high-ranking scholar, his mother the daughter of a minor court official. His father had seen her in the market and had to have her so he brought her into his household as a concubine. His father's first wife had only borne girls, so when Han Jin was born, his father made a deal with Han Jin's mother and his wife. Officially, Han Jin was listed as the first wife's child giving him the right to serve the court and to inherit. However, as she is the true mother of his only son, his mother ranks first in his father's heart.

Needless to say, the wife enraged, jealous, has always treated Han Jin's mother no better than a slave, humiliating her at every opportunity. And while she has mostly neglected Han Jin, she's also discouraged any relationship between him and his mother. Han Jin's father has turned a blind eye to all this as his wife's father is a court minister and it would be politically disadvantageous to make her any unhappier than she already is.

Han Jin ended his story there, though Shin Seo could tell there was more; words Han Jin couldn't or wouldn't say out loud. They sit there, silent, awkward, Han Jin's mother a shrouded presence.

In the silence that followed, Shin Seo, eyes closed, let his mind wander, considered the man in front of him and what this man might be able to do for him. Finally, looking at the floor between them, he said, almost to himself, "I would like to learn how to read and write."

Han Jin could barely hear Shin Seo's request, has to replay it in his head a few times before he can understand what Shin Seo is asking of him. When he finally understands, Han Jin is delighted; he thinks it's an excellent idea, something he is certainly capable of doing, and quickly agrees.

For his part, Han Jin didn't ask Shin Seo any questions about his life knowing that his story will unfold in its own time as Han Jin earns his trust. They agree to meet the next evening at dusk in the warehouse before parting ways.

The sun is just setting as Shin Seo exits the warehouse. Reds and oranges giving way to green and cyan before the stars emerge in the darkening sky; their light a distant memory piercing the illusion of time. Shin Seo feels a calm presence he can't understand—somehow he knows that he isn't alone, that he's protected by someone, something, as his life unfolds. He begins to hum quietly to himself as he carefully finds his way back to the market where he takes his time wandering through the streets, taking in the array of colors and smells as though they were brand new to him before heading back into the woods.

There isn't much he's ever envied anyone, but he has always envied others' ability to read and write. It has always seemed so mysterious and beautiful, the characters dancing across the page filled with hidden meaning to all but those infused with the knowledge of their ways. The marriage of brush, ink, and paper; fleeting thoughts immortalized.

As he walks, it's as if a door has opened and he's stepped through it to a larger room than he has ever imagined himself in. He moves at a relaxed even pace, breathing in the emerging life around him, letting go of the bindings placed on him at birth.

Freedom smells sweet.

As he walks up the hillside, his hand reaches into his jacket for the stone Chang Mi gave him, it's smoothness adding to his sense of well-being. He doesn't know how long this feeling will last, but he's going to savor it for as long as it does, feeding on it to fortify him for any coming struggles. There are sure to be struggles ahead, but in this moment all that matters is feeling his strength and knowing that all is right in his world.

Somehow, he finds himself sitting on the river bank. He closes his eyes and listens to the movement of the water, listens to the owls and crickets and other sounds of the night. As he opens his eyes, a star falls from the sky, and then another. Stars are racing across the sky before disappearing into the blackness of a moonless night. He doesn't understand it, but senses its perfection. He is learning that life can be filled with more pleasure than pain.

He takes his time bathing in the cool mountain water before heading for home. It seems odd, but in this short time, he has come to think of the cave as home.

When he arrives everyone is asleep except the father.

Shin Seo sees that the mother has put aside some dinner for him. He also notices that there is a growing stock of herbs and mountain vegetables. He adds his purchases to the store before sitting down to eat. Between mouthfuls, he tells Tae Moon about the meeting with the yangban. The father is wary, but also realizes that having a young noble on their side could be useful.

They leave it at that and go to their beds. The father joining his family, adds himself to the three bodies merged as one. Shin Seo, his nest empty until he nestles into it, imagines himself walking through the market reading all the indecipherable signs and banners as he drifts into sleep.

UKRAINE 2

The night is pitch black with no moonlight, no guiding stars. Rivka and Hannah's eyes have adjusted some, but not enough to keep them from stumbling and bumping into things as they pick their way through the field. Rivka has tied a rope she found in a barn from her waist to Hannah's so they don't get separated.

Navigating the uneven earth is difficult as they are newly blind. Up until a short time ago they walked in the world of the sighted, the pitfalls and obstacles before them were visible. Now they must rely on newly forming senses.

They seem to be going better when suddenly Hannah hears Rivka stifle a scream, hears her mother drop to the ground, as she feels the tug of the rope.

Briefly, Rivka sees stars, the stars that come with the unimaginable pain of the barbed wire tearing through her eyelid. She can feel the blood, in her eye, on her face. How could this happen? She indulges in her tears, lets the black mood overtake her, oblivious to everything except her pain and frustration.

Hannah doesn't understand what happened, but she can sense the seriousness of the moment. She quietly sits down, careful not to disturb her mother, and waits. She senses her mother's silent sobbing. Hannah wishes she could comfort her mother just as Rivka comforts her, but she knows it won't work. She starts singing a song Rivka often sings to comfort her as quietly as she can to herself. *Tumbala tumbala tumbala laika* . . .

Finally, the pain subsides a little, the bleeding stops and Rivka is ready to continue. The black night is just beginning to turn morning rose and she can see a barn not too far off. Hannah has dozed off and Rivka gently wakes her. She takes Hannah's hand and they make their way to the barn, stealing themselves away in a corner and settling in. When Hannah finally looks at her mother's face, she bursts into tears. Rivka pulls her onto her lap and rocks her, comforting herself as much as her daughter. *Tumbala tumbala tumbala laika.* She begins to sing quietly as she strokes Hannah's hair. Together they lay down and drift into sleep, Hannah curled up in her mother's arms, as the sun rises over the fields.

KORYO 4

Shin Seo awakes with tears in his eyes though he doesn't know why. Such strange dreams, though he can't recall any details. He quickly dries his eyes, not wanting Chang Mi to worry. Fortunately, she's busy with the baby while her mother prepares breakfast. He gets up and stretches all the sleep out of his muscles before stashing his bedding away. Preoccupied with his own thoughts, he quietly leaves the cave to go wash up before breakfast.

Walking toward the river, he absentmindedly pulls the stone from his belt, turns its smoothness over and over in his hand. When he reaches the stream, he becomes aware of what he's doing and brings the stone to his cheek, feels the warmth it has absorbed from his hand and imagines Chang Mi's gentle hand on his cheek. He spots her father and quickly returns the stone to his belt.

The sky is thick with clouds, rain imminent. They wash just their faces and return to the cave where breakfast and Chang Mi are waiting.

Just as they enter the cave the sky lets loose, the rain drenching the earth. At the first crack of thunder the baby begins to wail. Tae Moon goes to him, picks him up and cradles him to his chest, his hand gently cupping the baby's head. As the father sways he hums softly and the wailing subsides; he is safe in his father's arms. Even when the thunder roars again, he remains calm. Shin Seo is impressed with the strength and tenderness of this man; confirmation that he had made a wise choice in staying with this family.

Without thinking he turns to Chang Mi who is busy helping her mother prepare breakfast. She seems so familiar, something about the look in her eyes, the way she smiles. Suddenly, she looks up and smiles at him, glad for his attention. Will I ever be able to tell him?

When she heard he was going to learn to read her heart skipped a beat. She was so proud of him, so happy for him. And then it struck her, why couldn't she learn how to read? Did she dare ask her father? She and Shin Seo could practice together.

At breakfast, Chang Mi sat between her father and Shin Seo trying to muster the courage to ask for the outrageous. But why exactly was it outrageous? Just because she was a girl? If slaves can find a way to be free, why can't girls learn to read? Still, sensing it might be too soon to ask she stayed quiet.

The rain stopped just as suddenly as it had begun. Shin Seo invited the father to explore the hillside with him. He was surprised at how well the father already knew their surroundings. They began to talk about their lives. The father had worked in the stables most of his life, at first keeping them clean, then learning how to tend to the horses, and eventually even how to train them. Tae Moon had taught himself to read key characters in order to better learn his craft, though he'd had to keep it a secret. His skills were rudimentary, his ability to write non-existent. Even so, Shin Seo was impressed.

As they walked and talked they discussed the best routes for escape, explored smaller more hidden caves, and what areas to avoid. Tae Moon had also seen the slave hunters, had also been determined to learn the area in order to protect his family.

And as they walk together, united in their purpose, mutual trust and respect grow between them along with a relaxed familiarity. To cap off their walk, each manages to catch a hare on the way back to the cave.

Thus they enter as brothers, proudly displaying their catch. Chang Mi can barely contain herself. As slaves they rarely ate meat. Now, she could savor its flavor, its texture twice in one week! Not to mention seeing her father and Shin Seo's relationship grow. As they eat their mid-day meal the air is almost festive, the seriousness of the adults had lifted letting the spring air into the cave.

After the meal, Shin Seo set off for his first reading lesson. The shapes of characters he could never understand dance in his mind's eye as he makes his way to town and the warehouse.

He's the first to arrive. In the center of the room where the crates were, there is now also a small rectangular table. He sits down and places his hands on the surface. With closed eyes he caresses the whole of it imagining the feel of paper under his palms, the brush in his fingers. When he opens his eyes, Han Jin is standing there watching him.

Han Jin is remembering how he resisted his lessons as a boy. And here is this man before him, to show him the gift he had been given. Without uttering a word, Han Jin carefully sets paper, brushes, water, ink stick, and ink stone before Shin Seo and sits beside him.

He had thought carefully about what characters to teach Shin Seo first, mulling over his own first lessons. Of course it was obvious once he'd figured it out.

Han Jin prepares the ink, grinding the ink stick into the stone in a slow circular motion, picks up his brush, carefully fills it with ink, and draws two characters. Shin Seo watches with rapt attention. Then Han Jin nods to Shin Seo to pick up the other brush and follow his movements.

Together they prepare their brushes carefully filling them with ink, laying hair on stone, turning, filling and shaping the bristles. Side by side their arms lift the brush—the brush poised above the paper in preparation for the first stroke, the tip coming down to meet the paper, a pas de deux between teacher and student, one sure-footed, the other clumsy.

When the dance is done, there are two characters on Shin Seo's paper.

It hadn't even occurred to him to ask what he was writing, but now, seeing his work, ugly as it is, the curiosity overtakes him. He looks at Han Jin, the question in his eyes. Han Jin smiles and tells him he's just written his own name.

Shin: god, being, faith, soul, joy mother, father

Seo: book

The tears come before he can stop them.

Han Jin's eyes too fill up, emotions overflowing. He feels the pride and joy of being a part of this moment, of having done a righteous act of no benefit to himself other than what he now feels. When Shin Seo is ready, Han Jin encourages him to continue to practice writing his name, helps him to perfect these two characters, encourages him to find the grace and beauty in the art of calligraphy.

Shin Seo is entirely focused on being able to bring out the meaning in these characters, of mastering each movement, each motion, from filling and shaping the brush to the thick and thin strokes that silently speak his name.

In the years to follow, Han Jin would often come back to this moment, to remember the determination of his friend in everything he set his heart to. It served both as a reminder of why he loved this man, and inspiration when he needed it. Undoubtedly, this was the moment that cemented their friendship and bound them together whatever might come.

Finally, Han Jin showed Shin Seo how to clean the brush. He rolled up the paper, including the clean, empty sheets, and carefully put them in the bamboo tube he had brought for Shin Seo. Then, just as carefully, he put the ink stick, ink stone, ceramic water bottle, and brush in the box cleverly crafted to hold them. Shin Seo was overwhelmed. What had he done to deserve such treasure, this new friend and these gifts.

Back home, the mother and baby are asleep, but Tae Moon had let Chang Mi stay up and wait for Shin Seo to return. Actually, there was nothing he could do to get her to go to sleep with her mother and so he had just given in.

Chang Mi insists Shin Seo show them everything as soon as he walks in. She grabs the box from his hands and opens it without even asking. As she places it on the table she marvels at the implements, picks up the brush and runs the tip over her palm. She looks up at her father, "Can I learn, too?" stunned that the words have come out before she could stop them.

Tae Moon is dumbstruck. Yes and No are fighting each other to be the answer so no words come forth. Though Shin Seo wants to offer to teach her, he holds back. Chang Mi looks down at the table, afraid of what her father's answer will be. Tae Moon slowly sits down beside his daughter, places his hand lovingly on her head, strokes her hair as he considers what to say.

It had never occurred to him, but was that because his skills were so rudimentary or because she's a girl? What harm could there be in it? And before he can talk himself out of it, he gently turns her head so he can look into her eyes as he says Yes.

Shin Seo quickly sits down opposite them, his excitement taking over, removes the paper from the tube and unrolls it on the table before them. He can't stop smiling. "What's it say?" Chang Mi is dying of curiosity. "What's it say?"

Very quietly, barely able to voice the words, he replies, "Shin Seo" with his eyes fixed on the up-side-down characters in front of him. The sheet is filled with the pairs progressing from pitiful, to almost graceful.

At his utterance, Chang Mi's childish enthusiasm turns serious. She feels like her heart is going to burst. Before her is the name she had chosen for her first-born, for the light of what once was her life. This Shin, this Soul she had brought into the world.

Shin Seo suddenly feels his mother's presence, tries to imagine her face had she been able to see what he had written. He looks up and sees exactly what her expression would have been. Shin Seo and Chang Mi lock eyes as the recognition and love pass between them.

In a flash, everything Shin Seo had been feeling around Chang Mi makes sense. He has no doubt who she was and it's clear she's known it almost from the beginning.

Abruptly, he rolled up the paper and put it away. He was too full to take in any more. Too full to even eat anything before preparing for sleep. Dazed, he left the cave to wash up, to settle down, to walk, to plunge himself naked into the cold water of the stream, to let the shock to his skin cover up the real shock he'd just received. He lay floating on his back, eyes closed, focusing entirely on the feel of the air and water on his skin, the wet support beneath him as he slowly, lazily moves his legs to keep them afloat. The cool brush of the air wafting across his belly, his chest, his lips and closed lids.

Finally, he opens his eyes and gazes at the star-filled sky. As he does so he hears a sound, like bees buzzing among the blossoms of the plum trees. He sees his mother take her last dying breath. And then, miraculously, he sees her take her first breath as she came back to this life. The images disappear as the buzzing fades away.

He dresses and walks home breathing in the smell of the woods around him, the sounds of the night replacing all other thoughts. He feels whole in a way he never has before. As he lays down, his bed prepared by Chang Mi before she went to sleep, he whispers good night and closes his eyes, his body still remembering the feel of water and air, brush and paper.

UKRAINE 3

One eye open, one swollen shut, Rivka wakes up unsure of what time it is. The light is filtering through the slats in the barn. It's obvious to her they'll have to stay put until her eyelid is better. What if they're found? How long can their meager rations last? They have some water left from the previous day, but not enough to even last through the night.

She closes her eye, hoping to fall back to sleep, to escape her thoughts.

As she drifts, not quite awake, not quite asleep, she can feel herself floating naked in a cold stream, the cool night air soothing her. It's a strange and beautiful feeling—one she's never experienced before—oddly calming and exhilarating at the same time.

Hannah emerges from sleep feeling a tenderness toward her mother she doesn't quite understand. Happy that Rivka's bruised face looks so peaceful, she quietly gets up so as not to disturb her. As silently as she can, she explores the barn.

She finds a cat curled up in a corner sleeping. She wants to pet its black and white fur, hold it in her lap, but she knows it will bolt as soon as she touches it. The cat half-opens one lid sensing its observer. Hannah remains motionless and the cat continues its nap.

Hannah curls up, face-to-face with this small furry being, wondering what cat dreams are like. She smiles as the cat's paw twitches once, twice, and settles down again. Unable to contain herself, very slowly, she reaches her small hand out and gently caresses the cat shoulder to pelvis, just once to see what will happen. The cat half-opens both lids, assessing the situation, takes a deep breath, and closes its eyes.

Hannah can barely contain her joy in this simple success. She tries again, one gentle silent motion, shoulder to pelvis. This time she's rewarded with the cat's rumbling purr. The cat stretches and rolls over still purring. Hannah takes this as tacit permission to continue. She closes her eyes, listening to the purring as she gently strokes the cat.

Lost in the softness of the moment, she's startled out of her reverie by the rough tongue of the cat licking her hand. It seems she's made a friend. Wordlessly, she asks the cat what her name is. What comes back is an image of a white rose bud. Funny that a black and white cat would be named Rose, she thinks. Rose gets up, stretches out her legs, and rubs her cheek along Hannah's leg as she walks out of the barn.

Hannah follows her out, opening the barn door just enough to slip through. She's blinded by the light. It's been at least a week since she's seen daylight. When her eyes adjust to the light, she looks around and spies what was the farmhouse. Its roof is gone, the walls charred black, the doorway gaping, doorless, the windows broken. It's a sad sight, but she's relieved. The years of chaos and fighting have taken a toll on the peasants.

Rivka wakes up, sees Hannah is gone and has to calm her initial panic, has to remember that Hannah is not a foolish child. Standing up, she looks around, sees the open barn door and heads for it. Pssst. Pssst. Hannah turns and sees her mother in the doorway. She motions for her to come out.

Rivka experiences the blinding shock to her one good eye, feels the same mixed emotions at the sight of the burned-out farmhouse. She hugs her daughter close and whispers a prayer of gratitude to the same god she had cursed the night before when she ran into the fence.

Hand-in-hand they walk toward the house, all their senses heightened. They are overjoyed at the discovery of a well and a small garden. The potatoes are still tiny, but edible. But the real treasures are the beets and young peas. They harvest enough for several meals, these sole-survivors of the carnage. Then they find a tub and carry it into the barn.

They fill the tub with buckets of well water and delight in washing up for the first time since embarking on this journey. First Rivka washes her daughter using fresh straw and a bar of soap they'd scrounged to carefully scrub her clean. Next she washes Hannah's hair. Her mother's rough scrubbing of her scalp has never felt so good, so loving.

Still naked, Hannah takes up the soap to return the favor. Oh-so-gently, she washes her mother's face with her small fingers, careful not to disturb the lid as she washes away the blood, then picks up the straw to scrub the rest of Rivka's body clean. Finally, Rivka removes the wig she wears as a modest Jewish wife so as not to arouse the passion of men, and let's Hannah scrub her scalp and wash her hair.

Once clean, they reluctantly don their filthy dresses, but take this opportunity to wash their stockings and undergarments before carrying the tub outside to dump out the bath water. By now, their stomachs are calling out to be fed.

They don't dare risk a fire or staying outside for very long. And so they take their freshly harvested meal in the barn. Rose quietly returns, curling up next to Hannah, she purrs quietly as she drops off for a nap. Rivka doesn't quite know what to make of this. But Hannah explains that Rose lives in the barn and is her new friend, all the while gently, mindfully, stroking the black and white fur.

Rivka is worn out. The days of walking, her throbbing eyelid. She goes to lie down. As frightened as she was and as painful as her eye is, Rivka feels an overwhelming sense of gratitude for this chance to rest, to bathe, to feel some small bit of normalcy.

To ward off the pain and worry, she focuses on this feeling, on the sweetness of the day, and tries to imagine herself adrift on the river again as she drifts into sleep.

KORYO 5

Shin Seo wakes to the sound of family, the smell of morning. Chang Mi is busy cooing to her baby brother, Tae Moon bantering with his wife as he sets the table, Chang Mi's mother dishing out the morning porridge. The sound of a gentle rain mixing with the smells of burning wood and cooking rice.

He quickly gets up, puts his bed roll away and joins them at the table. They chatter happily during the meal as if their situation were nothing out of the ordinary. After their meal Shin Seo is restless to go out, to walk, to take in the magic of the forest.

Walking through the woods, He's absorbed in the smells left behind by the rain—wet bark, soaked earth, blossoms promising the fruit to come; and the sounds, birds calling, searching each other out, wind dancing with the trees; and in his own thoughts as the letters of his name still dance before him.

It's not long before he comes upon an abandoned, terrified fawn, it's leg broken, eyes wild at his approach. Tears well up in his eyes at the distress of this beautiful, pitiful creature. Even so, he knows that this is a boon for him and the family. He sits down and places his hand on its shoulder and looks deep into its eyes, hoping to calm it down. Then slowly, carefully, he strokes its neck, positions himself so that it can lay its head in his lap. Quietly, he begins humming and the fawn relaxes, lays its head down, closes its eyes, and spends its final moments in peace.

He remains sitting with the lifeless fawn, taking in the preciousness of life. He waits until the silence enveloping the moment dissipates and the life around him finds its way back into his world before standing up. He lifts the fawn up onto his shoulder and takes it home where they will make good use of it.

He arrives at the cave where Chang Mi is busy practicing the characters that make up Shin Seo's name with a stick in the dirt. She jumps at his approach and in the process wipes out the writing. Shin Seo doesn't understand her alarm until he sees her mother come out, the baby tied to her body, chiding Chang Mi for not getting her chores done.

Tae Moon appears and takes the fawn from him. This is a first and everyone is excited. There will be plenty for them to do, from butchering and curing the meat to tanning the hide.

After assisting Tae Moon with butchering the fawn and scraping the hide, Shin Seo once again takes his leave. With him is the bamboo tube and writing box, their straps criss-crossed across his chest.

A steady drizzle accompanies him on his walk into town. The green leaves are iridescent, the birds the only noise-makers. When he hears the crack of a fallen branch behind him, he turns and easily brings down the boy who, rock in hand, was ready to attack.

The boy can't be older than twelve or thirteen. As Shin Seo kneels beside him, his hand holding down the boy's chest, he carefully looks around to see who else might be there. He spies several boys running back up the hillside.

The boy has the same wild, frightened look the fawn had. His clothes are ragged and he's clearly not had enough to eat. He lifts his hand off the boy's chest and, before he can ask any questions, the boy is off and running to find his friends. If he didn't have an appointment, he would have followed. He'll have to find their nest another day.

As he heads into town he carefully goes over the strokes he's learned in his head, his hand following. Walking through the market, he slows down at the book stalls imagining the day he buys his first book, the characters no longer indecipherable.

He can't quite shake the image of the boy, eyes wild, frightened and hungry. Difficult as the serfs' life was, at least he'd had his mother looking after him, food to eat, adults to depend on. How could it be that the people who had everything, who were supposed to take care of those who fed them, didn't even see them as human beings. The nobles were supposed to protect the people in exchange for the right to rule, the right to unimaginable wealth. Instead they seem to have created only despair and poverty, to only feel contempt for their charges.

Lost in these thoughts he arrives at the shed. His mood is dark as he enters and greets Han Jin. Han Jin

looks at him confused by the dour greeting. Shin Seo
tells Han Jin about his encounter with the boy. They sit,
both looking down, Han Jin feeling ashamed, Shin Seo
working to hold back his anger. Finally, Shin Seo looks
up and smiles at his friend. Perhaps he'll understand the
world better when he can read and write, when he gets
to know the man sitting beside him better.

Han Jin, still embarrassed, returns the smile, eyes
slightly downcast. He takes a deep breath, pulls a book
out of his jacket, and places it before Shin Seo. It's a writing primer. On the first page are the twelve basic strokes
he must learn along with simple words, characters, that
form the base of other words. For each character there is
also a key showing the order of the strokes and a picture
showing its meaning.

Silently he studies the first few pages, marveling at
the ingenuity of it, and a bit overwhelmed at the enormi-
ty of the task. When he looks up, Han Jin has prepared
the paper and writing implements. He hands Shin Seo a
brush, and shows him each stroke, tells him its name. Shin
Seo, with as much confidence as he can feign, copies each,
repeating its name until he can produce it with some ease.
Finally, Han Jin has him produce his first word:

man, person

Shin Seo is astounded at its simple beauty, his curiosity aroused, a sense of confidence quietly budding.

As they cleaned their brushes, Shin Seo opened up a

little about how he spent his time as a boy—the chores and seasons of farming, roaming the woods with his brothers, preparing flax for spinning. In many ways it was a good life. But when his father had to leave for corvee duty, or when there was a drought or floods and the crops were destroyed, food was scarce, disease rampant, taxes still owed.

Han Jin, afraid he might break the spell, just listened, hungry to know this new friend.

Shin Seo falls silent, a little embarrassed at his outpouring. Han Jin answers with a small smile. He wonders aloud whether the karma the Buddhists professed was true spiritual law or just a way to justify the inequity of their lives.

The moment when he recognized his mother reborn as Chang Mi floods Shin Seo's inner vision. He doesn't know the answer, but knows it's an important question.

Han Jin suggests that perhaps they should continue their evening with some wine and snacks. And so they find themselves sitting at a nearby tavern, talking with the ease of old friends though their lives couldn't be more different.

Shin Seo still hasn't mentioned where he's living or with whom. But he manages to broach the subject of run-away slaves. He's curious as to what a small family could do to keep from being caught and killed or returned to a cruel, child-molesting master. There were only three options Han Jin could come up with. Become the slaves of another family or for the government, leave the country, or live in hiding indefinitely.

Though it was the answer he expected, he had hoped for something different. He quickly drank his cup and then another before filling his friend's cup.

They'd been living together in the cave for less than a week, but already they were his family. It was up to him to figure out what they should do, but he didn't even have a hint of a plan. At some point he would have to tell Han Jin and enlist his help.

As if in tune with his sudden melancholy, the skies unload torrents of rain, holding them captive in the tavern. Before long, Shin Seo is drunk, Han Jin tipsy. Both are lost in thought, comfortable in their silence. Suddenly, Shin Seo looks at his friend and smiles, happy to see he's still there, before his head lands on the table.

Han Jin is at a loss. He doesn't know where Shin Seo lives and it will soon be curfew. He can't take him home; there are too many eyes, too many people reporting to his father and his father's wife. He gathers their things, lifts his friend up onto his back and takes him back to the warehouse, clumsily laying him down on some straw mats before leaving.

Shin Seo in a state between waking and sleeping is in a world familiar, yet completely different. He sees young women, girls, being rounded up and put on strange wagons.

UKRAINE 4

Hannah wakes feeling dazed from a dream she can't quite capture. Rose has curled up against her and is gently purring. Hannah smiles absently while stroking Rose's side. She's still trying to remember her dream, but all she can recall is a cacophony of sounds, strange writing, nothing more.

It's odd to wake in the same place. She's startled by Rose's rough tongue on her hand, then pleased. She wonders if it will be this easy to make friends in Chicago.

She looks over at her mother who is waking up. Astoundingly, Rivka's eyelid, while still red, is no longer swollen. Slowly, she opens her eyes, wincing slightly. They both sit up amazed. Hannah goes over to her mother and they embrace, relieved, overjoyed at this miracle.

They eat their breakfast leisurely. After just two more nights walking they should be able to cross the border into Romania. Then they can travel by day, not having to worry about soldiers finding them. Both are absorbed in thought, trying to imagine the days ahead. Hannah closes her eyes trying to imagine the ocean, the vastness of it. Rivka is trying to imagine being married again. She remembers him as a quiet industrious man, but that's about it.

They spend the day resting until it's time to pack up the food they've harvested and continue on their journey.

The night air is humid and warm, smelling of the rich earth. Rivka hums quietly to herself as she walks with Hannah's small hand in hers. Though her feet are sore, she takes pleasure in walking on this beautiful night. Hannah is awed by the star-filled sky and the symphony of the night creatures. How quickly the strange becomes normal, the normal strange.

They walk for hours until Hannah begins to stumble with fatigue. Then Rivka finds them a small abandoned shepherd's shack where they can sleep until dusk.

KORYO 6

His head pounding, Shin Seo wakes not knowing where he is. Slowly, he gets his bearings and sits up. He's got to get back to the cave before they go out to look for him. Quickly, he gathers his things and heads back, breaking into a run as soon as he gets to the woods. Finally, he arrives, breathing heavily.

The table is set for breakfast, but Chang Mi has refused to eat until he arrives. When he does arrive, she refuses to look at him or speak to him. Breakfast passes in silence, which suits him since his head is still pounding. Tae Moon lets him be. It's not his business where Shin Seo has been.

Breakfast finished, Shin Seo retreats to the river to wash up. It's raining. Not the downpour of the previous night, but a soft gentle rain. The kind that accompanies you on your walk with the music of the raindrops on the forest floor, gentle enough that the birds still sing. A warm nourishing rain bringing calm and wonder despite his pounding head.

Lying on his back in the river he reviews the previous day's events. He still has no plan for the future. There's time before it turns cold and they have to leave the shelter of the cave, but time is a slippery thing.

Does he dare tell Han Jin about the family? He doesn't want to live on the run, nor does he want that kind of life for Chang Mi. On the other hand, if they don't continue to escape the eye of the slave catchers, they'll end up back where they started or dead. Might Han Jin know of somewhere or some way they can live a decent life? Before he makes any decision to tell Han Jin, he'll have to consult with Tae Moon.

As he swims back to shore, the image of the boy, wild and frightened, appears on his inner screen. What can be done with those homeless, parentless boys? One thing at a time, first figure out what to do with myself and the family, then I can think about the boys' plight.

Walking back, the rain stops leaving only the scent and the wet of the earth behind. The sun emerges as the clouds scatter into blue. When he gets home, he'll share last night's lesson with Chang Mi if only to see her beautiful smile again.

But when he gets there, Chang Mi is busy sewing with her mother. She's learning how to repair the holes in her father's jacket. So Shin Seo invites Tae Moon out for a walk. He tells him what he knows about Han Jin, both his life and his ways. He tells him what choices they have, letting it sink in before continuing. Finally, he suggests that he'd like to tell Han Jin of their situation and see if he knows of a place where they can all live. Tae Moon simply says he'd like some time to consider it and they let it go for the time being.

55

When they return, Chang Mi is playing with the baby. Shin Seo asks if she'd like a writing lesson. She jumps up, runs over, and embraces him. The wait since her father told her she could learn has been intolerable.

Side-by-side they sit at the table An Jin has crafted. Shin Seo opens the box, takes out the writing implements, and then opens the tube and takes out the paper and the primer.

If he were to die that night, he would die a happy man. Being able to partake of Chang Mi's joy in learning to write is enough. He vows to buy her a brush, ink and stone, and some paper of her own. He won't be able to afford the box or tube, but that's OK, just that much is more than either of them ever dreamed of.

Together they practice filling the brush with ink and the basic strokes. Both are quietly content, absorbed in the pleasures of brush on paper. The promise of the world unlocked. When their strokes cease to improve, their fingers cramping, they stop and clean up. Chang Mi goes off to help her mother prepare the afternoon meal.

All through their lunch Shin Seo, in his mind's eye, continues to practice his writing. Afterward, he lingers at the table, letting the characters in the primer imprint in his memory. Finally, he unrolls his bed and lays down for a nap, the characters adrift behind his closed lids as he drifts off to sleep.

MANCHURIA 1

Numb. She feels nothing but numb as she walks through the remains of the camp; the rain making everything a blur. Perhaps it will blur the memories of the last three years. Perhaps it will wash away the pain and self-loathing.

She doesn't understand. Her living hell is suddenly empty of its devils. Only the women who served as the receptacles to their filthy desires remain; lost, confused. Them and the dead soldiers.

All at once, the numbness gives way to despair as she falls to her haunches and sobs herself to sleep.

When she wakes, she's curled up in the mud. The rain has slowed to a drizzle, the sky still a uniform gray reflecting her inner landscape. She can still smell the burnt flesh from the final battle. She smiles at the image of the devils running away from the Russian onslaught, suddenly weak and helpless; those not fleeing foolishly running towards certain death rather than face the shame of returning to Japan defeated. Odd to choose death over home, she thinks.

Home. The thought of home has become an unbearable longing felt in the depths of her being. Will she be able to go home? Will she be able to face her parents? Are they alive? She doesn't even know where she is, only that she came by land and it's not Korea.

Unexpectedly, her view is blocked. Someone squats down and sits her upright, pushes the muddy hair from her eyes and gently wipes her tear-stained, mud-stained face. She is lifted to her feet and the two women embrace, each crying silently on the other's shoulder, slowly swaying in each others arms.

The drizzle stops and the sky brightens though the sun is still obscured. Hand-in-hand they walk to the river, take off their clothes, and immerse themselves in the water.

Bathing in the cool embrace of the river, her ordeal seems like a far-away dream. Floating, eyes closed, arms akimbo, supported by the water, the warm breeze on her skin feels like freedom. And yet, an acrid taste remains. Her bruised body still aches. And her heart longs for an unrecoverable past.

Suddenly she feels the heat burning her flesh as the sun bursts through the clouds. She swims back to shore and finds a shady spot to wash her filthy kimono. Her friend is quietly humming by her side. It's the same song her mother would sing while doing chores. The tears return. She continues to scrub, to beat her kimono against the flat river rock. The silent tears become a moan, then a wail. When it turns to screaming her friend takes her into her embrace, holds her head to her heart. "Shhhh. Shhhh. It's alright. We're alright. Shhhh." She closes her eyes and an eerie calm overtakes her.

Her friend sits her down on the rock and hangs the kimonos on the tree branches to dry in the sun. Sitting next to her, her friend gently lays her head in her lap and strokes her hair. One of them has to remain strong. One of them has to keep them moving forward.

They begin to talk about home. They arrived together, both having believed they were coming to work in a factory with decent pay. They hadn't really known each other before, but now they rely on each other as sisters. Most of the others from their town either died of disease or infection, were shot or beaten to death, or killed themselves rather than endure a woman's greatest indignation again and again and again. Somehow, these two had hung on until the end, had managed to survive.

Talking of home is bittersweet. They talk about the food, their families, and the sheer beauty of the land, the sound and smell of it.

Finally, their clothes are dry. They get dressed and walk back, ignoring the bodies along the way. The Russians have stripped them of anything of value.

They reach the mess hall hoping there's some food left and find that they're late. The other women got there first. Even so, there's a bit of rice and some millet. They even manage to find some potatoes hidden in the corners. They find a bag and fill it with whatever is left. The journey will be long and what little script they were given is worthless. They go to their rooms to pack their few belongings.

Shin Ae removes her cotton print kimono and puts on the hemp hanbok she arrived in; a short pale blue jacket with a long white skirt. She can't help thinking about her mother as she puts it on. Her mother made all the clothes for the family, sometimes sewing late into the night. She looks at the perfectly even stitching on the seam of the skirt. With both hands, Shin Ae brings the soft worn hemp to her cheek and, closing her eyes, breathes in her mother's scent, smoky from the cooking fire, earthy from the fields.

Jinju arrives with her bundle and sits on the floor. She too has changed into her hanbok. Shin Ae smiles, happy to see her friend, happy to be leaving this place. She finishes wrapping her things into the bojagi, the cloth used to carry just about anything, carefully tying the knots. They divide the food into two bundles and each wrap the bundles of their belongings and the food into a single bundle which can be strapped to their backs.

Jinju has talked to one of the Chinese women about where they are. They seem to be about 150 miles north of the border in Manchuria, a spanse once a part of their homeland. They decide to return the way they came, following the train tracks so they don't get lost.

The freedom to walk away is both exhilarating and disconcerting. It doesn't help that they don't actually know where they are. Neither has been allowed to go beyond the confines of the barbed-wire fence since they arrived. Though one night, not long after arriving, in a fit of despair and bravado, Shin Ae tried to run away.

She was lucky that when the guard caught up to her, her only punishment was being hit in the back with the barrel of a rifle. The soldier hit her as if he thought she was a baseball he was trying to knock out of the park. Despite the pain, despite her inability to sit up unaided, she was put back to work the next day.

They pass silently through the gate holding hands; there is no one to stop them. Tears of joy flow freely, spontaneously, as they take one last look back. Walking toward the train tracks, the physical sensation of freedom, of once again owning their own bodies, begins to overtake the ever-present ache that went hand-in-hand with their servitude.

It's August, the trees are green and flowers are in bloom and, for the first time in years, they can take in the beauty of it. They have no need to talk as they walk along the railroad tracks. Each knows the other's heart. Each is testing the taste of freedom, of the possibility of happiness.

After several hours, they decide to break for a small meal. They spread the bojagi that hold their belongings on the ground for a table and each takes a potato from their store. Absorbed in their thoughts, tired from walking, they don't notice the soldier until he's kneeling beside them. Until just before he falls over exhausted and starving.

Though he's wearing a Japanese uniform, they can see that he's Korean, trying to get home like them. They let him sleep awhile before waking him. They let him devour the potato they give him before asking any questions.

Han Sa had been a medical student in Japan before being conscripted into the army. In the last days of the war he had deserted, hiding in the forest as the Russian bombs fell. The only food he'd had was what he could forage when he was bold enough to wander through the woods. To be caught by the Japanese would have meant instant death.

His story told, their meager meal consumed, they continue on their journey. There is no need for them to tell their story, he knows it all too well, it would only be a cruelty to ask them to say it out loud.

The women are relieved that he's familiar with where they are and can be their guide on their journey. They're also surprised that he knows what they've done and still speaks to them with respect as if they really had just been doing the factory work they'd been promised. He offers to take them as far as Seoul, from there they can easily find their way home to Hongcheon Village.

Han Sa is a pleasant distraction as they walk. He has a uniquely Korean sense of humor that they've missed. For his part, keeping the conversation light masks his awkwardness around these women. He's still not sure how to view them, how to relate to them, not only because of the life they recently led, but also because of the difference in class. When it comes to men and women and class, little has changed in their world.

And yet, Han Sa has changed. His understanding of what is important, of who is important, has changed. And so he holds off judgment and focuses on how grateful he is to have two beautiful traveling companions.

Finally, as dusk approaches, they find a village with a train station where they, along with many others on their way home, find a spot on the floor and lay themselves down to sleep.

KORYO 7

As Shin Seo begins to wake, Han Jin enters his thoughts. It seems he remembers something, but can't quite catch it. Once the baby starts crying, any lingering memory disappears. It's a desperate wail, unceasing and then, silence. Shin Seo, though not quite awake knows something is terribly wrong. And then the wailing starts again, only this time it's not the baby, but his mother.

Shin Seo sits up and sees the mother clutching her lifeless child. Tae Moon is trying to comfort her, to take the child from her arms, but she is inconsolable. Chang Mi is lost until she sees that Shin Seo is awake. She goes to him, curls up with her head in his lap, the tears falling silently; the two of them do their best to go unnoticed—witnesses to this tragic scene.

Finally, the mother falls silent, falls to her side, curled around her baby. Tae Moon can only sit by her side stroking her hair as she stares blankly, unable to see the world of the living around her.

As if nature were also in mourning over the loss of this barely lived life, torrents of rain begin to fall in sheets and waves. Nothing can be heard but the falling water.

As if God knew of no other way to show Its love in this moment of immeasurable sorrow.

After what seems an eternity, the rain lets up and Shin Seo quietly leads Chang Mi out of the cave so that her mother and father can be alone, so that Chang Mi doesn't have to see her mother in this state. They wander aimlessly through the forest until Chang Mi asks him to take her into the town. Shin Seo hesitates, but Chang Mi is insistent as only a child can be, and he relents on the condition that she stay by his side at all times. Nodding her head vigorously she takes his hand and begins to pull him along before he reigns her in.

They arrive at the market just as a crowd is gathering to see the traveling theater. Chang Mi tugs on Shin Seo's hand while longingly looking in its direction and he takes her over, holding her close to him, as the tight rope is being put up. The drummers are winding through the crowd, dancing as they beat out their rhythm. Chang Mi is enthralled, her body wants to dance, but she knows she mustn't stand out. Shin Seo is behind her, his hands on her shoulders so as not to lose her. He's grateful for this distraction, but can't relax for fear she'll be spotted by a slave hunter.

The drummers have made their way back to the center of the crowd, spiral dancing before moving off to the side and sitting as the dancers make their way out to the center of attention. It's a dance of joy and wonder as the dancers slowly turn like birds ascending, their sleeves trailing in the air around them.

Just then, Han Jin appears next to them. Chang Mi looks up at this handsome stranger. They smile at each other, instant collaborators. Shin Seo isn't quite sure what to make of this, but mostly he's pleased that the two most important people in his life have met and seem to have taken a liking to each other. They refrain from talking and focus on the spectacle before them, oohing, aahing, laughing, and clapping as if there were nothing strange at all about these three individuals standing together.

After the show, they make their way to their make-shift schoolhouse stopping along the way to buy some steamed buns, rice balls, and a couple of brushes and some paper. Chang Mi is having a very difficult time trying to stay quiet and calm as she eats these. She wants to jump and skip and sing her joy. Until she remembers her mother and brother. It's her first time experiencing such mixed emotions.

As they enter the warehouse, Chang Mi feels slightly let down at how shabby it is. She hadn't really known what to expect, but it wasn't an old run-down warehouse. Shin Seo brings over a crate for Chang Mi. They sit side-by-side facing Han Jin and Shin Seo introduces Chang Mi to his teacher.

Han Jin isn't prepared for this impromptu meeting, for a second student. But he's very pleased to get one more glimpse into Shin Seo's world, to be trusted with a life so obviously dear to him. He also now understands Shin Seo's questions about run-away slaves.

Han Jin takes out the paper, ink, stone, and brushes.

Chang Mi blushes and looks down as he hands her the brush he bought her. He decides that they should spend their time practicing the basic strokes. Shin Seo has improved, but some of the strokes are still awkward.

Shin Seo and Chang Mi practice silently, their whole attention on their task, while Han Jin observes, periodically praising or correcting their form.

After some time, Chang Mi's enthusiasm for writing the same strokes over and over begins to wane. While Han Jin is focused on Shin Seo, she begins to sketch his face, starting with his eyes, moving to his nose, and just as she begins his mouth, he notices what she's doing. Chang Mi quickly turns it over, embarrassed. But Han Jin comes around the table, insisting on seeing it.

Han Jin was shocked at how well this young girl had captured his features; especially since this was her first time using a brush. When pressed, Chang Mi admitted that she would often draw in the dirt using a stick, especially since they moved into the cave where there was very little to do all day. Han Jin didn't yet know how, but he was sure this could be a way for her to gain her freedom, or at least a life worth living. But since he doesn't have an actual plan or even a real idea, he says nothing about it as they pack up the paper and brushes.

Chang Mi holds Shin Seo's hand as they wind their way through the streets on the way back to the woods. She thanks him, though there is no need to do so. He just smiles and squeezes her hand. His head is swimming in thoughts so he doesn't have much to say.

The closer they get to the cave, the slower they walk.
When they finally arrive, they're stunned by the wall
of grief they're met with. Tae Moon is sitting next to Chang
Mi's mother trying to get her to eat some porridge. She
is still lying down, eyes unfocused, a low wail emanating
from her throat. He looks up at their approach. Chang
Mi sits down next to them and strokes her mother's hair,
tries to soothe her. But her mother makes no indication
that she's even noticed her daughter.

Chang Mi lies down with her mother, curling up
against her as best she can with her small body. She begins
to rock her, at first gently, then more and more fiercely
as she begins to sense that her mother is disappearing,
that it may not just be her brother she's lost. Chang Mi's
tears come as she urges her mother to return, and as the
rocking becomes more fierce, her pleas become more
urgent, until finally, Tae Moon gently pulls his daughter
away and holds her in his embrace, calms her as best he
can. He too is sensing that he's lost his wife.

Holding Chang Mi in his lap, feeling her warmth
and the special bond they share, he senses that he's not
entirely unhappy at the passing of the baby. Though he
would gladly have raised him as his own, he would always
be a reminder of a past Tae Moon hopes to break free of;
of a man he wishes he had never known. And navigating
their precarious path is difficult enough, let alone with an
infant. But he would truly grieve at the loss of his wife.

Shin Seo quietly goes about preparing the evening
meal. After stoking the fire, he goes out to get fresh water

for stew. He's fairly certain that Tae Moon hasn't had anything to eat and he's happy to have something to do. The fresh evening air and azure sky are a welcome contrast to the heaviness inside the cave and he takes his time.

Filtering through his thoughts are memories of his family and what it felt like to lose them one by one over the years. First was his father. Perhaps that was the easiest. Not because he didn't cherish his father, but because they only heard of it when the other men from the village came back from military duty and let them know that his father wouldn't be coming home.

He remembers his mother, squatting outside the house scrubbing his sister's clothes. She just kept scrubbing, rhythmically rubbing the cloth against the rock and itself as if she hadn't heard; the only evidence the tears streaming down her face. With three children, what choice did she have but to keep going. She spoke of him infrequently, but when she did it was with a tenderness that somehow embarrassed Shin Seo. Rather than ask her when he wanted to know more about his father, he would ask the other village men for their recollections.

He barely allows the memories of his brother's death to surface. The plague that took him and half the villagers was too horrible to dwell on. Shin Seo still feels the loss of his best friend and co-conspirator. To dispel the memory, he focuses on the light filtering through the leaves and the sploshing of the baskets of water suspended from his shoulders.

Entering the cave, he sees that Chang Mi has begun preparing the vegetables. He sets the water down beside her, pleased to see her composed again. Her mother is sitting up, though her eyes are still vacant. It seems she's eaten a few bites of porridge. Shin Seo and Chang Mi prepare the meal in silence with love and a sense of gratitude towards life which seems both odd and fitting.

When Shin Seo and Chang Mi finally sat down with Tae Moon to eat, they were all surprised that in this den of grief, they were eating one of the most delicious meals any of them had ever had. It was difficult to break the silence, but at last Tae Moon spoke thanking Shin Seo, reassuring Chang Mi, and asking them where they had been. After spending the day with a living corpse, he needed to talk, to listen, to feel the life in them.

As Chang Mi speaks of their adventure, she can't help but get excited again. She jumps up to get the paper from their lesson when she sees her mother, still motionless, and stops, hesitates, feels herself deflating. A little less enthusiastic, but undeterred, she brings the pages to her father and sits next to him, burrowing into his side so that his arm comes down around her shoulders as he studies her lesson.

At the sight of her brushstrokes, tears well up in Tae Moon's eyes spilling the banks of his lids. The well of mixed emotions is almost unbearable. Unconsciously, he strokes Chang Mi's head as he looks at how beautiful her brushstrokes are. He doesn't know if they are really masterful, or if it's just a father's pride, but even he can see that her strokes are confident and consistent. When he comes on the painting of Han Jin he's confused and asks her how it got mixed up with her writing.

69

"You have a very talented daughter," Shin Seo explains simply. Tae Moon stares blankly at Shin Seo, speechless. He can't take it in. Instead he pulls Chang Mi close and quietly tells her it's time to go to sleep. She begins to protest, but stops when she sees her mother out of the corner of her eye.

Silently, she goes over to where her mother is still sitting and gently lays her down. Then she prepares the bedding for Shin Seo and her father, before preparing her own and lying down. Her thoughts are chaotic as she closes her eyes. Images of her mother, the dancers, and Han Jin all fight for her attention as she drifts into sleep.

MONGOLIA 2

Mongke wakes with a disturbing memory of enemy soldiers in strange uniforms, defeated and strewn about. And then it's gone. The dream is replaced with the excitement of the coming day. He jumps up and goes to wash his face with the water his sisters have already fetched.

Outside the ground is muddy from the night's storm. It seems more rain is to come. All around the camp, boys are preparing to face the tests they must pass in order to join the men as soldiers on the next campaign. Mongke gathers his bow, spear, and leather vest, then mounts his horse. He takes one last look at his mother standing in the doorway. Their eyes barely meet before each looks away and he's off to the training ground.

He ignores the other boys arriving and surveys the field, clearly imagining all that he will be asked to perform. Finally, the men arrive. The ram's horn is blown and the boys dismount from their horses and assemble before the men. Mongke feels the butterflies in his stomach, the slightly weak feeling in his knees. By the time they are divided into four groups of ten the feeling has shifted from nervousness to excitement.

The groups are taken to opposite ends of the training ground. The boys will be tested individually, in pairs, and in mock battle. First they will be tested on their skill with the bow. If they don't pass that, it's over. Mongke purposely positions himself to be the first.

Once on his steed, he takes a deep breath before taking off at a gallop. He lifts his bow from his horse's side, pulls an arrow from over his shoulder keeping the target in sight, draws the arrow back, aims, releases, wheels his horse around to see the result. Yes! One down, nine more and he'll have passed the first test. Mongke knew all he needed to do was get the first and the rest would follow.

After the tenth arrow hit its mark, he rode to where the rest of his group were waiting. He doesn't notice the bloodied blister on his thumb, he only feels the joy of success and the rush of nerves and confidence. He barely notices the light drizzle as he waits for the others to finish.

By the end of the first round his group numbers eight. His confidence builds as he passes through each test. Finally it's time for the mock battle. Seasoned warriors fill in for the boys who have failed to advance. There are two groups of ten on each side with a warrior assigned to lead each group of ten in mock combat.

He checks his lance and readies his shield. The two sides face each other from opposite ends of the grounds. By now another downpour has just ended and the field is pure mud. He's wet and muddy, but it makes little difference to him.

Mongke looks around and realizes that he's the smallest rider but tries not to let it shake his confidence as he listens to his leader give them orders. Suddenly, an image of his mother comes to him and, for just an instant, he waivers. Perhaps he shouldn't be in such a hurry. Perhaps he should wait another year. Just as quickly he shakes it off in time to hear the horn signaling the start of battle.

Mongke is surprised at how disoriented he is in the me-lee and fails to hear his leader order a retreat. Then, without even understanding how it happened, he finds himself on the ground. He barely manages to get back on his feet and remount so as not to get trampled, he doesn't notice that it's blood he's wiping out of his eyes.

And then, just as quickly as it began, it's over.

He's disappointed and, surprisingly, equally relieved to learn that he failed. It was over for him when he missed the order to retreat.

His father meets up with him and wordlessly hands him a cloth to tie around his bleeding head. Mongke can't tell if his father is disappointed in him or not, but assumes he is; the shame spreading like a cold blanket.

After tying on the cloth, he turns and races off to be alone. His tears are indistinguishable from the rain hitting his face. He doesn't even realize he's crying until he slows his horse at the edge of the woods, the horizon turning orange and yellow as he and his horse enter at a walk. When he finds the right tree, he stands on his saddle and climbs onto the sturdy branch, the ever-waiting arm of a silent listener.

Only then does he let loose his emotions—sobbing with all his being—the wail of a young boy trying to be a man. It wasn't until today that he had any sense of his own mortality, that he felt just how small he is.

It was dark by the time he climbed back down onto his horse feeling empty and spent. He rode home slowly, reluctant to meet his family, reigning in his horse to a walk in the hope that the evening meal would be finished by the time he arrived.

He entered the yurt quietly, trying to be invisible, eyes cast downward to avoid seeing the reactions of his family. He especially didn't want to look at his mother's relieved gaze.

Without a word, he prepared his bed and lay down to images of horses moving pellmell around him as he struggles to get back on his feet, back on his horse. Finally, through sheer will, he forced himself to turn off all the thoughts and pictures and sleep.

KORYO 8

Shin Seo comes out of his dream with a sense he's had the same dream before, a feeling of strangeness and familiarity. He sits up, rubs his eyes, and looks over to where the family is still sleeping. He's grateful that he can slip out and spend some time alone.

He decides to take a different path to the river, curious what he'll find along the way. The air is still crisp, the trees draped in dew. Bird song fills the forest, long melodious songs, short staccato calls, and everything in between leaving very little room for silence. When he arrives at the river he wastes no time stripping and plunging into the cold water.

Once the initial shock wears off, he feels alive in a way he can only feel when his skin is braced by the cold wet of the river. Lying on his back he scans the cloud-filled sky trying to make meaning of the puffs of white. A dragon embracing a rabbit captures his imagination, gets him thinking. He wonders if it could be some sort of sign and decides to take it as a good omen. Rolling onto his belly, he swims upstream back to where he entered the water.

He has no idea what the day will hold. These days, every day seems to bring a lifetime of experiences. A year ago he could not have imagined his life today. As he dress-es and heads back to the cave he rolls the possibilities of what life will be like in a year around in his mind. He can feel what it might be like, but he can't see it.

Heading back, he takes each step as if he were walking into this new world and is suddenly in a magical clearing, the rays of the sun filtering through the clouds, reaching down to the earth. He stops to take it in. To bask in this feeling—in this moment, and continues on enveloped in its splendor as if draped in a coat of light and wonder.

When he enters the cave he has to work to not be brought down by the atmosphere. Chang Mi is just set-ting the porridge on the table while her father is trying to get her mother to even sit up, to engage in some way with the world of the living. Finally he gives up and joins them at the table.

Chang Mi asks him if she can join Shin Seo again. Tae Moon is concerned about her getting caught or in trouble, but he can't bear for her to see her mother in this state so he agrees to let her go. They won't be leaving for several hours, so in the meantime, she and Shin Seo agree to practice writing together and learn new words from the primer.

Shin Seo has mixed feelings about taking her with him. He had been enjoying his freedom and felt the bur-den of protecting her out in the world. But he also loved watching her delight in all the new experiences yesterday and is willing to do anything to help her and her parents. It's been years since he's had a family, the responsibility of it makes him feel like he's part of something bigger than himself and he's grateful for it.

As soon as he finished his porridge, Tae Moon slipped out for a walk to take a break and gain strength from the stunning beauty of their surroundings. It was all too obvious that his wife had no interest in continuing to live. She hadn't really wanted to run away, was too timid to be comfortable with it. Perhaps she blamed him and Chang Mi for the baby's death. Otherwise, he really couldn't understand why she wouldn't choose life, for Chang Mi's sake if nothing else.

When Shin Seo began clearing the table, Chang Mi curled up into her mother, laid her head on her mother's outstretched arm, draped the other lifeless arm around her shoulders pretending that it was her mother's will. She burrowed in tight against her, wrapped herself up in the woman who, up until a couple days ago, loved her, hoping it would ignite some spark and turn this empty woman into her mother again.

When that didn't work, she turned and began to smother her mother's face in kisses. Desperate for a response, she began to shake her mother, to yell at her as she began to sob. Finally, when he couldn't take it any more, Shin Seo gently tore Chang Mi away from her mother and held her briefly to calm her down before setting her to the task of preparing the ink.

He had already laid out the paper, brushes, water, and ink stone. He studied the primer as Chang Mi worked the ink on the stone. When she was done, he set the primer before them: *mother, father, child.*

77

母親
父親
兒童

Silently, each took up a brush and began to copy the characters. The intensity of their circumstances made it all the more important they learn well; helped their hands find the rhythm of the strokes; helped them portray the love and sorrow contained within the pictograms.

Tae Moon stopped at the threshold watching them, afraid if he entered, he would break the spell. Silently, in awe of the picture before him, he sat on his haunches and blessed this moment of respite for his daughter, for himself—the view of his disappearing wife obscured.

The scream that reignited the wailing caught them off-guard. Tae Moon ran to his wife, more to quiet than comfort her—how can you comfort the unconsolable. He pulled her to him, trying to bury her sobs in his shoulder as she beat her fists on his chest, grabbed his hair, screamed, and cried before collapsing, lost to them once again.

Chang Mi, tears streaming down her face, sits down next to her father where he draws her to his side. She's clearly shaken, as is he. Holding her and stroking her hair he doesn't feel so useless. The warmth of his body, his touch reassures her—she is loved by at least one parent.

Shin Seo, a part of, yet separate from this family clears the table as unobtrusively as he can, absorbed in the memory of his mother, remembering how she grieved at the death of his brother. But no matter how deep her grief, she never abandoned them.

When they saw him get the fire going, Chang Mi and Tae Moon joined him to prepare the meal. None could bring himself to speak, yet they took comfort in each other's presence, in the shared experience of preparing a meal, in the mundane tasks required to live in this physical world.

As the time approached for Shin Seo and Chang Mi to go to their lesson, Tae Moon wished he could join them, wished he could escape the hours to come with the woman who was once his wife, while simultaneously, all the reasons he can't leave her alone run through his head. He consoles himself with gratitude for having been able to take a walk in the woods, for having watched his daughter deftly wield the brush as she learns to write, for the meals he shared with her and his new friend. And in the end, he sends them off with a glad heart, anticipating the stories they'll bring back to light up this darkened cave.

As they venture out, the sky is overcast, the air heavy with the possibility of rain. Suddenly, Chang Mi wraps her arms around Shin Seo, burying her face in his belly. Awkwardly, he completes the embrace, cradling the back of her head in one hand, the other holding her trembling back. Slowly, hesitantly, he bends his head down and kisses the top of her head. Without a word, she releases her hold, wipes her eyes, and takes him by the hand, to continue on their way.

As the first drops fall, they make themselves known only by the voice they give the leaves above them. There's a magic to the sound of a gentle rain quietly falling amongst the trees. And the colors discover an intensity they hadn't previously known. Every so often a few drops would find their way to splatter the tops of their heads, their noses, their eyelashes. In this way, Chang Mi and Shin Seo made the transition from their shelter to the world at large; as if the earth were taking them into her healing embrace.

As they near the town, the sounds of the market begin to mingle with the sounds of the forest and Chang Mi, tossing her grief aside, grows excited again. She loses patience with their slow, steady gait and tugs at Shin Seo's hand to hurry him along.

As tempted as he is to let her excitement take them over, he reigns her in. They can't afford to get too comfortable, to stand out. It breaks his heart to have to stem her enthusiasm, but he doesn't know what he'd do if she got caught. She feels his fear for her, his love for her, and slows down just before they enter the town and head for the warehouse.

Han Jin is already there pacing in anticipation of their arrival. He can't contain his smile at the sight of them. He's not sure who he's happier to see. Perhaps Chang Mi since he wasn't sure she'd be back.

Once inside Chang Mi can hold back no longer and runs to the table where the paper, brushes, and ink are all laid out for them. She wants to show off the characters they learned earlier in the day. So she and Shin Seo wield their brushes while Han Jin proudly watches. Both are catching on quickly, though Chang Mi clearly has a better command of the brush.

Then he places a book before Shin Seo. It's not a primer, but an actual book. Shin Seo looks up, confused. Han Jin tells him that a scholar learns to read this book before ever being allowed to pick up a brush and write. Shin Seo looks into his lap, embarrassed. What does he, a lowly peasant, have to do with scholars. Suddenly he feels foolish for ever having asked to learn to read.

Han Jin feels an awkwardness between them he hasn't felt since the evening Shin Seo ran into the orphan in the mountain. Chang Mi looks up from her writing but doesn't understand why there is this tension between the two men. She looks from one to the other noticing the difference in their dress, their posture, and remembers that she is a slave, a run-away slave, and understands. At the same time, she knows the three share an unusual bond and, to break the tension, says, "If I—a slave, a girl—can learn to write, why can't you learn to read the classics?"

Han Jin holds his breath waiting for Shin Seo to respond. Shin Seo, eyes closed, takes in her words, tries them on and tests the feel of them. Then, slowly he raises his head, looks at his friend with a new light in his eyes, and says, "Why not?"

Han Jin feels the tears well up as he lets out his breath. He doesn't quite understand why he is so moved. A landscape of joy, embarrassment, and relief wash over him. He invites Shin Seo to sit with him opposite Chang Mi to begin the lesson, leaving Chang Mi to her own devices.

And so begins Shin Seo's study of Confucius, Han Jin reading the line and Shin Seo repeating it until he has it memorized.

大學之道
在明明德
在親民
在止於至善

The way of the Great Learning lies in letting one's inborn luminous virtue shine forth, in renewing the people, and in coming to rest in perfect goodness.

Absorbed in their work, in the great task of learning, they lost track of the time until Chang Mi informed them it was time to stop. "I'm hungry. I want to eat with my father."

What she doesn't say is that she wants to see if her mother has come back to her senses.

The rain has stopped and the night is clear and cool. They walk back stripped of words, each filled with their own thoughts and images; Shin Seo's head filled with the lines he had memorized, Chang Mi's with the feel of the brush and the magic of ink on paper. They barely notice the amazingly star-filled sky until they both see the shooting star arc across its dappled darkness. They stop to savor the moment and the good it might portend before continuing on, their eyes now scanning the sky as they go.

At the entrance to the cave they stop and peer in to assess the mood. Tae Moon is sitting next to his sleeping wife stroking her hair and humming softly to her. As they enter he looks up and smiles. He's been looking forward to hearing about their lesson, to feeling their warmth.

He had fixed dinner in anticipation of their return. The men sit as Chang Mi brings the stew and rice to the table. Once they begin eating, Chang Mi blurts out, "Uncle is going to become a scholar!" Tae Moon nearly spits out his food watching Shin Seo blush. "I'm just learning how to read," Shin Seo explains. But then shyly, with a touch of pride, he recites the first of the memorized lines, "The way of the Great Learning lies in letting one's inborn luminous virtue shine forth, in renewing the people, and in coming to rest in perfect goodness."

Tae Moon smiles as the thought comes into his head that life is going to become very interesting. He almost feels as if they're living outside of time in an era where anything could happen, even a peasant becoming a scholar. A laugh escapes his lips and he lets the thought go. Shin Seo looks at him quizzically, then, suddenly imagines himself in a scholar's robes and hat. "Nonsense," he utters to himself and breaks out laughing.

In an instant both men are laughing uncontrollably, tears running down their faces, as Chang Mi simply looks on confused and delighted. When they regain their composure, Chang Mi asks what was so funny, but neither can give her an answer. She gives up and continues to fill in her father on the afternoon's events until she begins to fade and he picks her up and carries her to bed.

As he drifts off to sleep, Shin Seo contemplates the line that he's memorized. He's confused by the gap between these lofty governing ideals of the scholars and the reality of their lives. Unable to reconcile the difference, he gives up and instead lets himself feel how incredibly grateful he is to his friend who is able forget that Shin Seo is a peasant even if Shin Seo himself can't.

It doesn't matter that he can't actually be a scholar; he can still learn. And why not learn something important.

And so he drifts off trying to imagine a life where he manifests virtue and abides by the highest good.

MANCHURIA 2

Shin Ae was the first to wake. Her sleep had been filled with dreams hovering between hope and despair and hope. She felt a sudden need to get out of the train station. Something about all these misplaced people made her nervous. As soon as she had gathered and tied up her belongings, she woke the others and went outside to wait for them.

She walked out onto the tracks and stared out at the unending trail of ties. She felt untethered, unable to conceive of where she was in space and time. Without thinking she began to walk, careful to only let one foot land on each tie. She was completely absorbed in her task so it was a surprise when Jinju and Han Sa appeared on either side of her out of breath.

She looked at Han Sa, not fully able to understand who he was or why he was standing there. Then her gaze landed on Jinju, her friend, and she felt the world coming back to her. Jinju gathered Shin Ae into her embrace. Stroking her hair she gently admonished Shin Ae for walking away without them. "You mustn't walk away on your own. How would we get on without you?"

All at once, at the sound of her friend's voice, Shin

Ae finally came back to her senses and explained that she was simply still a little groggy from sleep. "Let's walk on for awhile before we stop for breakfast," she suggested, leaving out that she desperately wanted to get away from the station, from all those people trying to get home.

Han Sa gently guided the women off the tracks. It was unlikely the trains were running, but he didn't want to find out what Shin Ae would do if they were.

It was hard to know what to talk about as they walked. Eventually, Jinju asked Han Sa to tell them about Seoul. But he couldn't find any words to describe it. Instead, he began to sing an old song that reminded him of home. Soon they were all singing. They took turns choosing the song, singing alone if no one else knew their song. It was the best way they knew of to talk about home without getting caught up in morose nostalgia for the lives they'd left behind.

It had been years since they could freely speak their language and sing their own songs. Imagine it, speaking your own language being a subversive act. The words felt fresh in their mouths, clean like freshly fallen snow.

When they sat down for breakfast, the words began to flow, as if cobwebs were being cleared from their minds, freeing their thoughts. They were able to joke, to tell the puns that come so naturally in Korean. They could laugh and be ridiculous. They could mock the Japanese who had lost so spectacularly after so many years of lording it over the Koreans.

None of them had known a life without the Japanese. In reality, for Han Sa there had been many benefits. Pri-

or to the war it had been difficult for him to understand why so many Koreans wanted the Japanese out of Korea. Before the Japanese, there were no railroads, no modern schools, it was unheard of for a Korean to study western medicine. But nothing could wipe away the horror of the last year spent on the battlefield with them. He could now fully rejoice in Korea's freedom.

For Shin Ae and Jinju it was different. They had both experienced the burdens imposed by the Japanese for very little benefit to the average Korean. But, now, they weren't sure life would be any better for them when they got back. Han Sa was an educated man. It was likely he would be able to go back to some semblance of his old life. They, on the other hand, were dirty. Who would ever marry them. And if they couldn't marry they would only be a burden to their families. They weren't sure they could even show their faces to their families.

As they continued on their way, rather than try to imagine their homecoming, they continued to sing and tell jokes. This journey home might be their last opportunity to hold their heads high, to not consider what others might think of them, to appreciate their freedom and each other.

The air grew hotter and dryer as the sun climbed. Han Sa guided them to the river where they could drink, cool off, and perhaps even catch some fish. Fortunately for him, the women were much better at fishing than he was and they managed to have a small feast. They spent much of the afternoon enjoying the river and each other's company, and even taking a short nap while waiting for the heat of the day to subside before venturing on.

KORYO 9

Emerging from his quickly retreating dreams, Tae Moon felt her absence before he opened his eyes. Sitting up he looked around the room, trying to remain calm. He went over to Shin Seo to tell him to stay with Chang Mi while he went to look for her mother. Instead, Shin Seo convinced Tae Moon to stay with Chang Mi, that he would go out.

Shin Seo stepped out into the chilly morning air. It had rained heavily overnight and the ground was saturated. He closed his eyes and breathed in the scent and coolness of it, clearing his head as he tried to picture where she might have gone; how long she'd been out. He kept seeing the river, so that's where he headed.

All his senses were alert as he walked the familiar path. Even the birds were unusually quiet as the sun struggled to show through the clouds. Regardless of his sense of dread, the beauty of the forest made his heart ache, the leaves filling in all the spaces where the sky used to show itself. Sweet pink and white flowers peaking through the forest carpet.

Dazzled, unable to suppress the joy that welled up

each time he walked this path, he looked for signs of Chang Mi's mother. He scanned the path, imagining her feet becoming cut and bloody as she made her way—she hadn't bothered to put her shoes on when she left.

Finally, he reached the river. Holding his breath, he walked toward the lump which could only be Chang Mi's mother lying at the river's edge.

She lay curled up on her side, motionless except for her long unbound hair floating in the water. The look on her face was not unlike the blank stare she'd had when awake in the cave, but her lips were blue, her skin pale. Without thinking, he sat down next to her and placed her head in his lap. She was soaked, shivering. She was still breathing, though no longer of this world. He stroked her hair and studied her face. It seemed she could see something he couldn't. And then, a smile came to her lips as she let out her last sigh.

Shin Seo closes his eyes and listens to the river. He wants to imprint her last smile into his memory so he can convey to Chang Mi and her father that her mother had died peacefully.

It was tempting to carry her into the river, let her float away, but he thought better of it. As he hefted her onto his shoulder he felt the weight of the grief that drove her to give up on her own life. How was it that her ties to her baby born of rape, outweighed her love for her daughter and husband? Perhaps it had nothing to do with the baby at all. Perhaps she had just reached her limit with this life.

The way back seemed very long. A cool misty drizzle

filled his senses. He felt as if he were in a dream where no matter how long he walked, he got no closer to his destination, so he was taken completely by surprise when he was suddenly in front of the cave.

Without thinking he carefully laid the mother's body down under the canopy of a tree. He took in a deep breath, and then another to calm himself before facing Chang Mi and her father.

He quietly entered the cave. It took no words for them to understand that Chang Mi's mother was dead. Her grief was still on him. "Where?" was all Tae Moon could muster. Shin Seo simply turned and they followed him to where she lay, the smile still caressing her lips.

Chang Mi turned and stormed back into the cave as Tae Moon bent over her, tears mixed with rain, and cradled her head in his arm, smoothed the hair from her face, bent his forehead to hers and wept. The silent tears turning to a guttural moan, the depth of pain in his belly trying to find escape.

Shin Seo left him and went to Chang Mi. She sat at the table stiff with rage. Shin Seo was at a loss, though on some level he understood her anger; she had been abandoned by her mother, betrayed. He sat down across from her. And there they sat, unmoving except for the expansion and contraction of their breathing. He sensed that some of her anger stemmed from some distant memory of pushing through her grief when her own child had died, when his brother had died, heeding the call of the living. It pained her to know how weak her mother had been. Her hero, her mother, her illusions shattered.

Finally, Tae Moon came in. He pulled his daughter onto his lap and held her, rocked her, repeating over and over, "We're OK, we're alright. We're OK, we're alright" until Chang Mi carefully kissed his face and agreed bringing him back to his senses.

Shin Seo and Tae Moon agreed that they should bury the body immediately and found a spot far enough away. Together they dug her grave using rocks to remove the dirt. Chang Mi squatted next to her mother's body and looked on impassively. After the men had finally placed the body in the grave, Chang Mi helped to fill the wet dirt back in and quietly said goodbye to her mother.

Once the hole was filled, together, on hands and knees, they smoothed the dirt into a gently rising mound and covered it with forest debris. When it was done each stood silently, as if alone, on the periphery, within the aura of melancholy and relief. Until Chang Mi turned away from her mother and went back into the cave to prepare a meal for those left standing.

Chang Mi prepared a meal filled with love and gratitude for the men who would raise and protect her. Even so, Shin Seo and Tae Moon could taste the salt of her tears in the rice, the bitterness of abandonment in the greens. But neither the tears nor the bitterness could hide the taste of hope in the stew.

They ate slowly, and with each bite their mood lightened so that by the end of the meal, they were ready to go out into the world and face whatever might come.

Without any discussion, it was decided that Tae Moon would join them for their lesson. Shin Seo lent him some fresh clothes and off they went, hiding their stores and belongings as best they could until their return.

As they approached the market, Chang Mi, as usual, couldn't hide her excitement—the people, all the items being sold in the stalls, both useful and decorative, and their destination. It was as if, though motherless, she now had three fathers.

Tae Moon felt caution and delight in equal measure—it seemed everyone was clear in their purpose, their place, except him. It seemed ages since he'd left the mountain forest, though it couldn't have been more than a few weeks.

Shin Seo was on alert as he shepherded them through the maze of streets, trying his best to avoid any soldiers on the way.

They arrived at the warehouse early. Shin Seo found an extra crate for Tae Moon to sit at the table while Chang Mi unpacked the brushes, ink stone, and paper. It was hard to believe that only a day had passed since they were last here. Funny how a lifetime can be lived in a day.

When Han Jin walked in, Chang Mi and Shin Seo were already at work with Tae Moon looking on.

大學之道
在明明德
在親民
在止於至善

The way of the Great Learning lies in letting one's inborn luminous virtue shine forth, in renewing the people, and in coming to rest in perfect goodness.

His arrival went unnoticed until he quietly sat down next to Shin Seo, curious to see if he'd made any progress. Chang Mi's father was surprised, and perhaps a bit taken aback, to see how happy Chang Mi was to see her teacher. He felt a pang of ineptitude. Other than getting her away from their rapacious master, what had he ever been able to do for her?

He stood and bowed from the waist before introducing himself to the noble who had given his daughter the gift of brush and paper. As her father, he offered his thanks to this stranger, though still hesitant to give in to his charm. In the presence of Han Jin's grace and generosity, Chang Mi's father felt shy, unsure how to speak to a noble who befriends runaway slaves and peasants.

They were the same age, Chang Mi's father perhaps a bit older, but Han Jin's social status demanded he be spoken to in formalities. His demeanor, on the other hand, said otherwise. Han Jin tried to clear up Tae Moon's internal debate when he responded with equal formality. A mix of emotions ran through Chang Mi's father as Han Jin shifted his focus to his friend.

Shin Seo feels like he has finally come home, like the four of them are finally reunited. Never in his life has he felt such hope, such ease, as if the pieces of the puzzle have finally started to fall into place. Surely it isn't just he and Chang Mi who have been together before.

No one spoke of the day's tragedy. The warehouse seemed a sanctuary, a reality far removed from that of the cave, except that one-by-one, all of the cave's surviving inhabitants had found their way into this new world. None could envision what it meant, their only option to be grateful for it, to give in to whatever it would yield.

Han Jin noticed that Chang Mi had copied the lines he'd given to Shin Seo. Already her calligraphy had a confidence that Shin Seo couldn't match. He set out paper and brush for Tae Moon, but on this evening, Tae Moon was content to watch his daughter at work, to marvel at her beauty, her intelligence, as she practiced her calligraphy.

After about an hour, Han Jin reads out the second line in The Great Learning:

知止而后有定
定而后能靜
靜而后能安
安而后能慮
慮而后能得

Knowing where to come to rest, one becomes steadfast; being steadfast, one may find peace of mind; peace of mind may lead to inner serenity; inner serenity makes reflection possible; only with reflection is one able to reach the resting place.

Shin Seo repeats the phrases as Han Jin points to each character until Shin Seo is familiar with each one. Then he shows Shin Seo how to form them.

Father and daughter both watch with rapt attention as Shin Seo and Han Jin perform their dance, Han Jin calling out the strokes, brush meeting paper, one graceful, the other awkward. Chang Mi, unable to just sit and watch any longer, begins to follow along. As Shin Seo and Chang Mi practice, Han Jin gently guides and corrects them, especially Shin Seo, adjusting how he holds the brush, his strokes.

As he watches, without realizing it, tears begin to slip from Tae Moon's eyes; he understands full well the gift being bestowed on his friend and daughter.

Chang Mi eventually tires of the characters and as memories of her mother begin to push their way through, her image makes its way to Chang Mi's brush. Her mother emerges from the paper picking wild vegetables in the forest near the cave, the baby tied to her back as she crouches beneath a flowering tree. On the next page, her mother is cooking over the fire, her back to the viewer, looking over her shoulder, smiling.

The men are all watching as she finishes the second drawing, speechless. Han Jin, not knowing of the morning's tragedy, only marvels at her talent while Tae Moon's heart feels like it's going to burst with so many thoughts and emotions pushing their way in and out. It was Shin Seo who broke the silence, "Let's stop for the evening. It's been a long day."

As they carefully cleaned and put away the implements and paper, Han Jin asked about Chang Mi's mother. "She's dead," Chang Mi answered matter-of-factly, just as if she had answered that she was home cooking dinner.

Tae Moon felt as if he'd been punched in the stomach, as if all the breath had been knocked out of him. He closed his eyes and willed himself to breathe, in out in out, as he reached over to embrace her. But she refused to be consoled complaining instead that she was hungry.

Han Jin worried about taking Chang Mi and her father to a tavern, so he offered to go out and bring some food back. Shin Seo said he would join him, eager for the chance to talk with his friend alone. Chang Mi was disappointed that she couldn't go out to the market with them, but accepted the reality and agreed to stay behind with her father.

At first, neither Shin Seo nor Han Jin knows quite what to say. They both start to talk at once, each then deferring to the other. Finally, Shin Seo describes his day—finding Chang Mi's mother on the riverside, carrying her home, burying her, and Chang Mi's anger. Han Jin is quiet, imagining the scenes in his head. "What now?" he finally asks.

"That's what I was going to ask you." Shin Seo stops walking and faces his friend, but Han Jin has no answer and they continue on their way. Shin Seo says they can continue to live in the cave for a few more months, but they need to find a better living situation before autumn.

Han Jin feels a knot in his stomach at the thought of them living like that, but he still hasn't devised a plan. Now that he's met Chang Mi's father and her mother is no longer with them, he should be able to figure something out. "I'll work on it," he says.

Han Jin buys some rice cakes and steamed buns and they head back in silence.

Chang Mi is delighted with the buns, doughy balls of steamy goodness, and fully immerses herself in the task of devouring as many as she can. The men, in contrast, are not very interested in the meal. Instead, Han Jin is learning as much about Chang Mi's father as he can in a short period of time to help him come up with a plan.

Eventually they notice that Chang Mi has fallen asleep and that it's time to part ways. Tae Moon gently wakes his daughter who seems to be talking incoherently in her sleep. It's dark by the time they head into the woods. They are silent and cautious, content to immerse themselves in the symphony and earthy scents accompanying the cool night breeze.

Back at the cave, they each make their bed, Chang Mi curling up against her father, and fall fast asleep.

UKRAINE 5

Rivka is the first to wake in the waning light. She marvels at her beautiful daughter's stamina as she prepares a light meal for them. She strokes Hannah's hair to wake her, wonders at the play of emotions over her face as she sleeps. Hannah wakes with an immense feeling of gratitude that her mother is there and wraps her arms around Rivka's waist as she lays her head in her lap. Rivka leans over and kisses Hannah gently on the cheek before unwrapping her arms and urging her to get up.

Tonight's dilemma will be how to cross the border. Surely there will be soldiers and they have no papers. Rivka decides that the answer will come when they need it. She's not sure if she believes in God, but she does believe in life, that life will provide what she needs.

As they walk through the night, a twinge of excitement begins to find its way into their steps; each step a little closer to freedom.

Sure enough, they approach the road just as dawn begins to color the sky and there's a dray stopped at the side of the road. A gentle but persistent rain has begin to fall and the farmer is rearranging the hay in his truck.

Rivka leaves Hannah hidden in the wood and cautiously approaches. He looks up and she smiles, asks in Russian where he's going. He's going to Dobrojani. Rivka tries to stay calm as she explains that she and her small daughter need to cross the border so they can be reunited with her husband. He seems sympathetic so she asks if he'd be willing to hide them in his truck, tells him she can pay him for the trouble.

He stares at her for what seems like a very long time, weighing his options, the risk, and finally nods. As soon as Rivka looks over, Hannah runs to her side and takes her mother's hand with both of hers. She's not nearly as trusting as her mother as she peers at the stranger.

He has them crouch in the front of the truck bed facing each other, leaning their sides against the wood that makes up the back of the cab. He stacks hay all around them, lays a tarp over them and the hay. The hay is prickly and itchy. They close their eyes against the dust and the dark, holding each other's hands to keep their bearings as the horses are urged forward.

Hannah falls asleep and dreams of her new life.

KORYO 9A

Still half asleep, Chang Mi reaches for her mother. The realization that her mother is not there brings her fully, brutally awake. She tries to fall back to sleep to avoid the emptiness she feels in her gut, but the chasm remains and instead of sleep, her eyes fill with tears. She buries her face in her father's back wrapping her arm tightly around his waist and sobs. Finally her tears subside as sleep returns.

Ukraine 5a

Rivka daydreams about the rest of their journey, the countries she's never seen, the ship, the modern world as she too finally succumbs to sleep.

Koryo 10

Shin Seo wakes still feeling the motion of his dream. He can remember nothing except that he's traveling with a child and the sound of falling rain. Before he can conjure any more, the fragments of the dream fade; only the sound of the rain remains. He opens his eyes, but they might as well still be closed—the heavy clouds have prevented the sun from reaching the pitch black cave. Chang Mi and her father are fast asleep, exhausted from the previous day's emotions.

The cool morning air is a shock as Shin Seo leaves his bed to peer out the mouth of the cave. The sun has risen, but the sky is black. Sheets of rain are falling, the wind periodically sending the cold wet into the cave. He stands there mesmerized, refreshed by the chilly spray soaking his face, his hair. Immersed in the sound, the briskness, the strange dark, he thinks of nothing; he just is. Without noticing, he begins to rub the stone Change Mi gave him between his thumb and forefinger.

Shivering in his wet clothes he comes back to his senses. Reluctantly, he leaves the mouth of the cave and lights the fire. He finds the water buckets and gets thoroughly drenched in the few seconds it takes to put them out to catch the rain. Within minutes, they are filled and he brings them in before changing into dry clothes. He measures out the rice, adds water and sets the pot over the fire to make porridge.

Before long father and daughter have joined him at the fire. They remain silent, staring into the flickering tongues of light, each absorbed in the beauty and mystery of the flames, their thoughts unfocused. Shin Seo slowly stirs the porridge, lost in the motion, the rhythm, as the boiling water begins to soften the rice. Neither Shin Seo nor Tae Moon wants to remember the heart-wrenching sobbing in the night. But it's hard to forget given Chang Mi's quiet, her lack of chatter, the smile missing from her face. What do men know about comforting a child?

Chang Mi gets up and sets the table for breakfast. It's cold away from the fire. She begins to shiver and the tears well up again; the tears soon falling as fast as the rain. Sitting embracing her knees, she rocks in rhythm to her cry, "Oma, why? Oma," starting off as a low moan, getting louder and louder until she begins to choke on her words, on her tears. The men can't stop their own tears. Tae Moon breaks himself away from the fire and takes his daughter in his arms, rocking her, kissing her head, pressing his cheek to the crown of his poor motherless daughter, the flow of his tears caught in her hair.

Shin Seo continues to stir the rice and stare into the flames, his heart aching for this little girl, for his own mother, the tears flowing, until it's time to take the porridge from the fire and ladle it into the bowls Chang Mi has set on the table. She's fallen silent again, the tears a mere trickle as she separates from her father to sit between the two men, to feel the comfort of their warmth, their love.

Quietly, in silent reverie, they eat their rice.

When they've finished their meal, Chang Mi kisses each man on the cheek and takes the bowls out to be washed by the rain. After setting them down, she stands face up to the sky, mouth open to drink in the rain. Arms outstretched, palms up, she begins to twirl 'round and 'round, giggling as she gets dizzy and finally falling down in the mud.

Shin Seo and Tae Moon are shocked then grateful to hear Chang Mi's laughter. Like magnets, they are drawn outside to her, the rain now falling slowly, the air warming. They stoop down to her and she paints a mud streak on each of their faces, finding it to be the funniest thing in the world. Her father paints her nose as Chang Mi places a handprint on each of his cheeks.

Just then, the sun begins to come through the clouds and Shin Seo sees the rainbow arcing above them. Staring at the arc of color painted across the sky, they can each feel how even in their sorrow, they are blessed.

The morning passes quietly.

Shin Seo leaves father and daughter alone and walks to the river. He doesn't take his usual path, not wanting to revisit the place he found Chang Mi's mother.

The trees are still dripping from the downpour, the smell of earth pungent, the birds singing their approval of the sun prevailing over the rain. As he walks—alert to the sounds around him, to any crack of a branch or cough or anything that might signal that someone is nearby—he tries to imagine their future. But every road is ultimately blocked by the fact that Chang Mi and Tae Moon are runaway slaves. Their only hope is Han Jin. Perhaps he has the power to forge new identities for them.

His thoughts turn to himself. What can he do? All he really knows is farming and fighting. Merchants need licenses to sell in the market. You need a house to run an inn. He shakes his head to clear it of all these impossible thoughts and breathes in the earthy air, focuses on the trees freshly clothed in green. He stops when he sees a frightened hare running across his path, hears the crack of a foot coming down hard on a fallen branch.

Hiding behind a tree trunk, he watches the boy

emerge, sling shot in hand chasing after the hare, and can't help but laugh. The boy, angry, looks up and recognizes the man he had once tried to rob.

Shin Seo stops laughing when he sees the state of the boy, skinny and filthy, his clothes even more ragged than when Shin Seo last encountered him. "I'll help you," Shin Seo says quietly, quickly, hoping to be trusted, "I'll show you how." The boy stares at him, unsure, looking like a frightened rabbit himself.

Shin Seo pulls his sling shot from his waistband. "I'll help you," he says again. The boy hangs his head and drops to his haunches, defeated, hungry. Slowly, carefully, Shin Seo walks over to the boy, squats down, puts his arm around him, and draws the boy's head to his shoulder. The boy sighs deeply and relaxes for what seems like the first time in his life.

Neither asks the other any questions about who they might be or why they're living on the side of this mountain. Shin Seo tests the boy's ability with the sling shot before teaching him how to get more power and better accuracy. Then they set about the task of bringing down a hare. They stand still and wait in silence until a hare finally comes along nibbling on the forest fare.

Engrossed in its task, the hare doesn't notice the hunters nearby poised to take its life. Shin Seo quickly takes his shot and the hare is down before it can react. The boy looks up at Shin Seo, a smile on his face, a glimmer of hope in his eyes. They retrieve the hare and wait for an opportunity to test the boy's newly learned skill.

He fails at his first attempt.

Shin Seo doesn't let him get deflated, but shows him how to do it better. Finally, on his fourth try he succeeds in bring down his prey.

They part ways, neither looking to be entangled in the other's life. Shin Seo is relieved to know that, though the boy and his friends will face many dangers, at least they won't starve. He feels a little lighter now as he continues on his way to the river.

The air has warmed. When he reaches the river bed, the clouds have been replaced by a deep blue sky. He removes his coat and belt and runs into the water. It's only been a couple days, but he misses it in that same way one would miss the embrace of a lover. He loves the wet of it, the feeling of floating, arms outstretched, eyes closed, weightless.

After a bit he opens his eyes to the vastness of the blue sky. Gratitude for his life wells up, overflowing his edges, expanding his boundaries until he feels as though he's floating through the sky, drifting above his body floating on the water until the fish, nibbling at his toes, abruptly bring him back to himself. He swims to the bank, scrubs his face, neck, and feet, then finds a large flat rock and lays himself out to dry.

When he returns to the cave, Chang Mi is quietly at work on a painting. Tae Moon signals Shin Seo to leave her be, not to break the silence. Tae Moon has prepared a simple mid-day meal for them, ready for whenever Chang Mi has finished. The men leave the cave so as not to disturb her with their talk.

Tae Moon explains that Chang Mi has been moody all

morning, caught between tears and laughter, between anger, sadness, and joy. Shin Seo relays his encounter with the boy. They each fall into their own thoughts triggered by the recounting of the morning's events.

Chang Mi emerges, hugging her father's leg as if to moor herself in a storm. "*Pogo shipassoyo.* I missed you," she says, almost shyly, to Shin Seo, looking up at him. Her father reaches his hand down to pet her beautiful hair and Shin Seo squats down to look into her eyes. It breaks his heart to see her looking so lost, her sparkle dimmed. He cups her face in his hands, forcing a warm smile to his lips, "I missed you too."

The three go in and have their meal. Shin Seo tells Chang Mi about the boy and the rabbits. "I want to learn," she whines. The men say nothing. "I want to learn how to use a sling shot!" The men are still speechless. She looks from her father to Shin Seo and back. "Teach me!" The men look at each other. Finally, Chang Mi's father shrugs his shoulders, unable to find any good reason to deny her. There's nothing normal about their life—she's a run-away slave, a girl impossibly gifted in so many ways—so why deny her? "OK." Chang Mi is beaming. Clearly she has the best father in the world!

Shin Seo sits down to practice his writing after their meal. Chang Mi is too excited to sit and write, so she goes out by herself to play, dancing and talking with made-up friends. When he's finished, Shin Seo decides to bring Han Jin to the cave rather than face the stress of going to town with Chang Mi and her father. Chang Mi is disappointed, but her father is relieved and she let's it go, taking satisfaction in her recent victory.

Shin Seo finds Han Jin already waiting at the warehouse. Though Han Jin is happy to see his friend, he can't hide his disappointment that Shin Seo is alone. Shin Seo teases him for a few minutes, before telling him that he's alone because he's come to escort Han Jin to the cave. Han Jin is surprised and delighted. He welcomes any opportunity to escape the stifling confines of the noble classes and is especially pleased to be trusted by Shin Seo and his newly adopted family.

On their way back, Han Jin insists they stop for more paper and a variety of brushes for Chang Mi. He wants to encourage her talent in any way he can. Of course he also buys some steamed buns, ostensibly to tide them all over until dinner, but really just to have the pleasure of watching Chang Mi's delight when she bites into one. While he's at it, he gets some sweet rice cakes for dessert. Finally, they head into the woods.

"I met the boy again," Shin Seo tells Han Jin. Han Jin reflects on the supposed order of their Confucian world. "If the scholars and nobles really followed the teachings, those boys wouldn't be living alone in the forest." Han Jin, ponders aloud his dilemma, he's determined to live the teachings but how can he respect those higher in rank than him when they're so corrupt, when they use the teachings only as a way to keep their riches and exploit those below them.

They fall silent, reflective.

The evening is warm and the sky clear. The trees are fully enveloped in green now. Each spring day brings changes to the mountainside. Nests are being built, soon there will be hatchlings needing to be fed. The intrigues of the world are hard to fathom against the industry and songscape of the birds.

Chang Mi is outside waiting. As soon as Chang Mi sees her teacher she runs to him, grabs his hand and pulls him toward their home. Han Jin can't help but be delighted at this warm welcome. Oddly, these are the only people with whom he can relax. She pulls him to the table her father made, excited to show him how well Shin Seo has done with his writing and also her most recent drawing.

In all the excitement he barely takes in that their "home" is a cave.

He's pleased to see how diligent Shin Seo has been and the progress he's made. But what he feels when he looks at this girl's drawing can't be put into words. The picture is of Chang Mi's mother sitting under a tree with the baby in her lap. Her eyes are closed and there is a sweet smile on her face.

He does not regret stopping for new brushes.

Tae Moon greets the yangban, still awkward, bowing from the waist. Han Jin responds in kind, he is not here as their superior, but as their friend. He gives the brushes to Chang Mi's father, not wanting the gift to be misunderstood in any way. "Thank you," says Tae Moon. "Someday I'll find a way to repay your kindness."

Chang Mi and Shin Seo have already set the table for

their lesson—paper, brushes, ink, ink stone, water. They call their teacher over, impatient to learn. Han Jin in turn calls Chang Mi's father to the table, encouraging him to join them. Tae Moon is reluctant at first, but finally gives in when Chang Mi gets up and pulls him over to the table.

物有本末
事有終始
知所先後則近道矣

Things have their roots and branches; affairs have a beginning and an end. One comes near the Way in knowing what to put first and what to put last.

They begin reciting the passage, repeating after Han Jin between bites of the steamed buns until it becomes familiar. Then he shows them the passage in the book he gave Shin Seo.

The students take turns reciting it the lesson as Han Jin points out each character. Once they've learned the words and the characters, they discuss the meaning. Finally, it's time to write. Han Jin carefully shows the order of the strokes for each character, then invites them to pick up their brushes and join him.

Han Jin had never planned on becoming a teacher. He can't begin to share with them the gratitude he feels to have these very unconventional students in his care.

For the first time in his life he feels a sense of purpose. It's strange, but he feels closer to these three than to his own family or anybody else for that matter.

Tae Moon and Shin Seo concentrate on their awkward strokes. It's a challenge to control the brush, to fill it with just the right amount of ink, to paint each stroke in the proper order and direction. While Han Jin guides her father and Shin Seo in their struggle to learn, Chang Mi easily masters the lesson and leaves the table.

She carefully prepares their dinner, a simple stew with fresh mountain roots and herbs, dried deer meat, and rice. By the time the meal is ready the savory scents have overpowered the men's ability to concentrate. The writing implements quickly disappear and the table is set for their first home-cooked meal together. Out of deference to this noble in their midst, to their teacher, Shin Seo and Tae Moon wait for Han Jin to begin eating before taking their first mouthful.

Han Jin is quick to praise the cooking skills of his prize pupil. She blushes, hardly able to contain herself. Her father, though bursting with pride, just smiles quietly to himself. The rest of the meal is quiet, each man lost in his own thoughts about their future; Chang Mi content to just be with them humming to herself.

When the rice cakes are brought to the table, Chang Mi squeals with delight. When she finally calms down and finishes her first mouthful, she asks her teacher to sing them a song. He chooses a favorite of his mother's. Chang Mi and her father follow with a duet. Finally, Shin

Seo has no choice but to take his turn. He turns to Chang Mi and sings her the lullaby she used to sing him as a boy.

Han Jin and her father don't understand the tears forming in Chang Mi's eyes even as she smiles. Chang Mi curls up with her head in Shin Seo's lap and allows this man who once was her son to lull her to sleep.

Tae Moon soon carries Chang Mi to bed and Han Jin takes his leave. It's been a full evening.

Making his way through the forest Han Jin's thoughts and feelings form a tangled web. Joy and excitement are all mixed up with sadness and trepidation. He's worried both for his cave-dwelling friends and himself, though more for them. So far, no one in his household knows what he's been up to, but his servant is bound to catch on at some point. If only he knew where his servant's loyalty lay—with him, his father, or his father's wife. He would love to have an ally, someone who could help him come up with a plan for Chang Mi and her father, but the risk is too great. One slip and they would be sent back to their master or worse.

It amazed him how comfortable he felt with them, even with the awkwardness between him and Chang Mi's father. They all seemed so familiar, like old friends or family. He thought about finding positions for them within his household, but didn't trust his father's wife. There must be some way to put Chang Mi's talent to use.

He took a deep breath trying to clear his head with the smell of the spring forest's pungent night air. The full moon appeared through a break in the canopy stopping him in his path. Frozen, transfixed, bathed in its light, Han Jin heaped his cares and desires onto the moon goddess. Then he took another deep breath, this time to let the moonlight reach deep into his lungs, to fill him with hope, to seal the deal with her to take care of them and watch over them whatever may be in store for them. Briefly he closed his eyes, "Please," he whispered, before continuing on to his father's house.

As he approached the house, he saw his servant waiting for him. "Where have you been?" he demanded.

"Walking in the forest. It's a beautiful night." With no further explanation, he brushed past the servant and went through the gate. Before retiring to his room, he stopped to wish his mother a good night's sleep. She tries to engage him in conversation, to learn what he's been up to. He wishes he could confide in her, but that would only put her in danger too and so he leaves her and goes to his room where the bedding has been laid out and the candles lit.

He sits at his desk, eyes closed. Images of the evening come and go. He reads a few pages before blowing out the candles and finally laying down to sleep, an uneasy calm settling over him as he drifts off.

MANCHURIA 3

Shin Ae, Jinju, and Han Sa emerge from their nap with vague memories of being together before, none of them able to articulate it. It was too strange to talk about anyway, so they each keep it to themselves, their bond deepening.

As Shin Ae and Jinju packed up their belongings, Han Sa noticed a pair of eyes watching them from behind a tree. As soon as the eyes were spotted, their owner ran off. Rather than risk frightening Shin Ae, he let it be.

They continued down the tracks, the air pleasant, the heat of the day behind them. But with the lovely magic of evening came the mosquitoes. The women were too busy fighting them off to talk. Finally Han Sa said, "Just ignore them." The women look at him, puzzled. "Just ignore them. They'll either bite you or they won't. You can focus on them and let them drive you crazy, or ignore them and enjoy the evening."

With those sage words he began to sing a song that was popular before the war began. Shin Ae and Jinju realize how ridiculous they must have looked fighting off the mosquitoes and laugh so hard they can barely stand. Han Sa stops and waits amazed at how quickly they can move from one state of mind to another like fast moving clouds passing over the sun. When they had regained their composure, he began the song again and they joined in.

In part, he wanted to bring the mood up because he knew the eyes were following them and he didn't want Shin Ae and Jinju to notice. But mostly, it was because he wanted to hear Shin Ae sing. She had one of those amazing voices that could transport you to other worlds, a voice that brought joy to the hearer's heart. And so eventually, Shin Ae was the only one singing, the other two more than content to listen.

After a couple of hours, they decide to find a good spot to spend the night. Once they are settled, Han Sa goes out to find some fire wood and see if he can find out more about the eyes that have been following them. Walking behind him, while the eyes are focused on the women, Han Sa is finally able to get a good look at him. He appears to be a Japanese soldier, but he can't be more than fourteen or fifteen years old.

Slowly, with the stealth he's mastered these past months, he walks up to the boy who doesn't notice him until Han Sa is standing next to him. The boy freezes, eyes wide, panting in fear. In Japanese, Han Sa tries to calm him, "Don't be afraid. I won't hurt you." The boy, relaxes a bit, but is still frozen in place. It's clear he deserted the Japanese army and has no place to go. Han Sa invites the boy to help him find firewood. Finally the boy takes a deep breath and follows Han Sa into the woods.

Han Sa understands that this boy will follow him

home if he let's him. He isn't sure if Korea is the best destination for a Japanese boy, but it isn't his decision to make.

Shin Ae and Jinju are surprised to see the young Japanese soldier following Han Sa with an armload of firewood. In Korean they ask Han Sa what happened and he explains. Shin Ae is watching the boy as they speak. She turns to him, and in Japanese asks him if he understood what they were saying.

He nods. In Korean she asks how he knows their language. He looks at his feet as he explains in Japanese that his mother is Korean. When his father's family wasn't home, she would sing to him and speak to him in Korean. But she told him he must never speak it or they would both be in trouble.

Shin Ae wraps her arms around the boy, her tears spilling onto his head. As relieve as he feels to be comforted, he wrests himself from her embrace, not wanting to be seen as a boy.

Together, they build the fire and prepare fish stew and a little barley. During their meal they agree that they'll have to teach the boy to speak Korean before reaching the border, and that he needs a Korean name. They agree on Jong Nam since he came from the east. Somehow now that Jong Nam has joined them, their little family seems complete.

While the women clean up after the meal, Han Sa coaxes Jong Nam to speak. His accent isn't good, but with Han Sa's encouragement he speaks a few sentences. He makes them all laugh when he tells them to sleep well and even sings a couple lines from a lullaby his mother used to quietly sing as he drops off to sleep. Shin Ae picks up where he left off and one-by-one they all drift off.

UKRAINE 5B

Rivka wakes to the sound of stern voices; the soldiers at the border questioning the farmer. She tries to hear what they're saying over the pounding of her heart. The voices are too muffled to make out from under the hay. Then the voices stop and they lurch forward. She sheds tears of relief and joy as she kisses Hannah's hands, presses them to her cheeks. The worst is over. Hannah, though still drowsy, perfectly comprehends, a smile spreading across her face as she drifts back to sleep.

After some time, perhaps an hour, maybe two, the cart comes to a stop. They can barely hear the farmer calling them out and quickly unbury themselves from their shelter of hay. Rivka can see that they've stopped just outside the village. With the farmer's help, first Hannah then Rivka, jump down from the side of the cart.

Rivka smiles her beautiful smile as a token of her gratitude, unsure whether to renew her offer of money or whether it would be an insult to his obvious generosity. Hannah, unable to help herself, overcomes her shyness and wraps her arms around his legs while quietly thanking him. Rivka takes this opportunity to gently put a roll of bills in his hand. He accepts her good will with a simple nod and offers to take them the rest of the way to the market. Rivka accepts trying not to jump out of her skin with joy and relief.

The man, glad to have some company, begins talking about his life. He tells them of his farm, his wife and many children, his worries with the instability of the times. Rivka and Hannah just listen as he tries to make sense of everything. Rivka can barely take in his words as her head is too filled with her own thoughts. Even so, she does her best to nod at appropriate times and encourage him to go on.

His story told, he asks Rivka where she's headed next. She explains that they need to find their way to the Belgian consulate in Bucharest.

As Russian Jews, they have no citizenship, they're stateless. To get on the boat for America, they'll need passports and the Belgian government is one of the few that will help them.

She knows that she needs to get to Kutchurgan or Tiraspol to catch the train, but isn't sure how to get there from Dobrojani. He offers to ask at the market if anyone is going that way.

When they reach the market in Dobrojani they agree on a place to meet after the market closes and part ways; each with a lighter heart than when they first met, each savoring the inexplicable intimacy of strangers.

Rivka and Hannah are tired and hungry. Mother and daughter wander through the market looking for some rolls and milk before finding a place to sit and eat under the stand of trees they had set as their meeting place.

Rivka finds it strange to be amongst people again. Here, at least, most can speak and understand Russian. She wonders how she'll be able to communicate as they venture closer to their destination.

Hannah is quite pleased with her transformation from a bat who flits about only at night to a human who enjoys the sun. She revels in the feeling of the sun warming her small face as she soaks in the activities of the market sellers and buyers. Unlike Rivka who drifts off now and again, Hannah is wide awake, taking in all the colors and shapes and sounds of her surroundings.

Finally, the man returns with a couple he's found for them. After the introductions, the man is eager to get home. Rivka thanks him profusely, wishing there was more she could do to repay him, but, other than the rubles she gave him, her gratitude is all she has to offer.

The couple are Bessarabian Jews with whom they can freely speak Yiddish. They live in Slobodzeia, south of Tiraspol, but offer to take Hannah and Rivka the whole way in their cart. What can Rivka do but accept and do her best to be good company for the five-hour journey. Hannah, on the other hand, content in her mother's lap, falls fast asleep and dreams of the strange life awaiting her in the New World.

KORYO 11

Han Jin wakes with the strangest images in his head. Odd foreign buildings, his whole being aching. The servant has a wash basin ready and he gladly douses his face, drying his skin hard with the hemp cloth, as if he were trying to rub off years of accumulated filth, to obliterate memories he can't quite remember.

To make up for his abrupt exit the night before, he has breakfast with his mother. They talk about his preparation for the civil service exam, the weather, various gossip around the household. His heart aches for her when she's summoned by the first wife who is no doubt jealous of her time with him, his affection for her, the true mother of the one and only son of the house.

His day is taken up with studying and visiting the garden where he tries to think up the impossible—a plan for his students' future—until, finally, it's time to go meet with them. He leaves his servant behind. Fortunately, this is nothing new. He's never really gotten used to being followed around and would go out by himself whenever he could.

He takes his time walking past the houses and through the market, paying close attention to all the people, particularly the merchants, servants, and peasants. He tries to imagine Shin Seo, Chang Mi, and her father finding their place there. What would they be doing? Where would they be living? Before they can do anything, Chang Mi and her father need forged identities. Suddenly, an idea comes to him. What if he were to set up a book stall and have them run it? They have a lot more learning to do, but still, it's the first idea he's had that has the right ring to it.

He takes a deep breath, closing his eyes. He can't quite see it, but he can feel it—feel them settled into a new life—a smile blooming as he opens his eyes.

For the first time that day he notices the deep blue of the sky, the puffs of clouds. He feels lighter. Suddenly, he can taste the aroma of the savory delights in the food stalls. He sees the image of Chang Mi oohing and aahing over steamed buns and heads to his favorite vendor to buy a dozen.

In his excitement to get to the cave, his head swimming in thoughts he can't quite catch, he barely notices his surroundings. Until he hears the shouting and the sound of running. Han Jin looks around until he finally sees the private soldiers, slave hunters. His heart stops. He spins around desperately looking to see who they're chasing after when he hears the crack of a branch, the thud of a fallen body. The soldiers in their haste didn't hear it. As quietly as he can, Han Jin heads in the direction of the fallen prey holding his breath, his heart pounding.

The woman looks like a frightened doe. He lets out his breath in relief to see it's not Chang Mi or her father but is shocked to see that he recognizes her; he's seen her in the market. Before he can do anything, the soldiers have descended. The only thing he can do is bear witness to her fear, to the hunters' indifference as they force her to stand, bind her waste and wrists with rope, and drag her away, stumbling and limping, her head turning towards him, her eyes pleading for him to do something.

His heart hurts. Her image plagues his thoughts for the rest of the way to his friends' shelter.

Once the cave is in view, he stops to compose himself, to let go of his feeling of powerlessness in the face of such brutality. He breathes in the forest air, looks to the canopy of green and through it to the bright blue sky. He closes his eyes to imagine the joy he will feel at seeing Shin Seo, Chang Mi, and her father.

Suddenly, Chang Mi's little arms are wrapped around his legs and he looks down to see her beaming face. The pain in his heart begins to melt as he reaches down to pick her up and carry her into the cave.

Once his eyes have adjusted, he sees Shin Seo and Tae Moon busy practicing the previous day's lesson. Their strokes are improving, but still lack grace. Still, the characters are recognizable if not beautiful. He feels a sense of pride at their progress.

Han Jin puts Chang Mi down and greets his friends now standing in front of him. They exchange bows and sit around the table. He pulls out the still warm buns from inside his coat and hands them to Chang Mi who quickly unties the bojagi to get to them. Showing great restraint, she walks to each of the men and offers him a bun. Each accepts his bun with feigned formality and a slight bow of the head. Finally she sits down and together they savor the warm, chewy goodness.

Then it's time for the lesson. He can tell them his idea after. He points to the first passage and asks Shin Seo to recite it. Shin Seo stumbles his way through it, Chang Mi quick to jump in where he gets lost. Then Han Jin has them all recite it together over and over until it flows with confidence. Finally, they write it with the smaller, finer brushes Han Jin has brought them.

The Way of Great Learning lies in letting one's inborn luminous virtue shine forth, in renewing the people, and in coming to rest in perfect goodness.

They move on to the next passage, repeating it until they recite it effortlessly before writing it down.

Knowing where to come to rest, one becomes steadfast; being steadfast, one may find peace of mind; peace of mind may lead to inner serenity; inner serenity makes reflection possible; only with reflection is one able to reach the resting place.

Finally, they study the third passage.

Things have their roots and branches; affairs have a beginning and an end. One comes near the Way in knowing what to put first and what to put last.

By the time they finish, Chang Mi has once again turned from writing to drawing. On the paper is Shin Seo and Chang Mi's father bent over their brushes, concentrating on their strokes. Han Jin tries to find something he can say to guide her, but her natural talent far outstrips his years of learning. If she had been born into nobility, as a man of course, she would possibly have had the chance to study with a master painter. Suddenly, the image of the woman caught by the slave hunters flashes before him and he turns pale.

Shin Seo sees the blood drain from his friend and teacher's face and wonders what's going on. He holds back from asking, knowing it's probably something that can't be said in front of Chang Mi. Instead, he asks if he'd like to stay for dinner. Instantly, Chang Mi jumps up and insists he stay. Though he's overjoyed at the invitation, Han Jin hesitates before agreeing. How can he take food from them? But to refuse would be worse.

Han Jin tells them to look at the next passage in the book and see what they can understand for next time. They carefully pack up the paper and writing implements before Chang Mi brings them rice, mountain vegetable stew, and dried venison. They all laugh at how surprised Han Jin is when he tastes the stew. He didn't know such simple food could be so delicious.

It's a quiet meal. Shin Seo and Tae Moon ponder the meaning of the words they've been writing; the words of scholars and nobles. They keep their thoughts to themselves, unwilling to show their ignorance. Han Jin is wondering what they'll think of his idea, but doesn't want to bring it up with Chang Mi listening. He's sure she'll love the idea and doesn't want her to be disappointed if her father doesn't agree. Chang Mi, meanwhile, is happily humming to herself, studying the men as she eats.

The meal over, Han Jin rises from the table and says his goodbyes. Shin Seo joins him, curious about what caused his friend to go pale earlier in the evening.

The moon is full in a cloudless sky, lighting their way through the mountainside. After walking for a few minutes Shin Seo finally asks, "What happened?" Han Jin looks down, listens to the crunching of his footsteps on the forest floor. "I saw a woman get caught by slave hunters; someone I'd seen in the market before." Shin Seo sighs deeply in response. They both know their days together are numbered if they don't find a way for Chang Mi and her father to live in the open.

"If there's no other way, I'll go back to the land and bring them with me."

"There's a way," Han Jin assures him. Shin Seo looks at his friend in disbelief. "What would you think about running a book stall? It will take some time to make it happen, but if you and Chang Mi's father are willing, I'll figure it out.

"Just think about it for now. If you like the idea, talk it over with Tae Moon."

Shin Seo is stunned. It seems so absurd, an impossibility, but he trusts his friend and he hasn't come up with any ideas of his own, so he agrees think it over.

They say their goodbyes and part ways, Han Jin heads to a tavern to cover his whereabouts with a few drinks before heading home, Shin Seo toward the river.

The night is clear and cool, filled with the activities of creatures awakened by the light of the moon and stars. Shin Seo is completely absorbed with the task of imagining himself a merchant, a book seller. Two weeks ago he never even imagined he'd ever learn to read. Suddenly, he trips over some roots and lands hard on his shoulder.

He sits up and moves his arm around, massages the pain he only half notices. Closing his eyes, he first imagines the stall to the left selling ceramics, to the right bolts of fabric, across the way ornaments. Finally, he imagines the stall filled with books.

He's standing in front of the stall. Chang Mi is there putting up one of her paintings, an image of trees in bloom on the mountainside. A woman comes by, inquiring about the price. They come to an agreement and Chang Mi hands her the painting in exchange for a coin. Then Chang Mi's father comes out from behind a stack of books, to replenish the display.

Shin Seo opens his eyes. Somehow he knows if he can imagine it, it's not impossible. That was how he got the courage to leave the farm. He gets up and heads back to the cave curious as to how Tae Moon will respond.

Before going inside, he stops and takes a deep breath to calm his excitement.

Chang Mi is fast asleep. Her father is sitting at the table pouring over The Great Learning memorizing their lessons. To Shin Seo, this seems to be confirmation that this wild idea just might be the answer. Tae Moon doesn't notice Shin Seo until he's seated at the table beside him. Looking up he's surprised and delighted to see his friend smiling at him.

"What?" he asks Shin Seo. Shin Seo says nothing, just laughs. "What?" he asks again smiling back at his friend. "That yangban has great faith in us," Shin Seo finally replies. Tae Moon waits for Shin Seo to continue. "How would you feel about selling books in the market?"

Tae Moon just blinks, wondering if he's heard correctly. "Don't say anything, just sleep on it and we'll talk in the morning." Tae Moon nods, stunned, speechless. Shin Seo pats him on the back and goes over to unfold his bedding. Lying on his back, eyes closed, he again imagines the stall in the market, this time imagining himself sitting at the entrance waiting for a customer to arrive as he drifts off to sleep.

MANCHURIA 4

Shin Ae's screaming wakes them up. Her dreams are still plagued with the imprint of her first night as a 'comfort woman'. Han Sa and Jong Nam are helpless in the face of her suffering, but Jinju has gotten used to it. Gently, she strokes Shin Ae's hair and face, cooing to her softly to wake up.

Shin Ae bolts upright with a start, finds her friend and hugs her desperately until the fear drains out of her and she falls back to sleep, her head dropping onto Jinju's shoulder. Carefully, with a love born of shared experience and compassion, Jinju lays Shin Ae back down. She looks over at Han Sa and Jong Nam with a wordless plea for them to understand her friend.

Perhaps because Jinju was older, she was able to endure the pain and humiliation better. Shin Ae was only 14 when she was rounded up, still a child not having even bled yet. A shiver went through Jinju, as if her body were trying to shake off the memories.

When Shin Ae awoke, she remembered dreaming of a cat and a barn but nothing more. She was surprised to see everyone up and the breakfast table ready. "Good morning. What a beautiful day," she beamed as she stretched and wiped the sleep from her eyes. Han Sa looked at Jinju confused, but Jinju only smiled and shrugged, grateful that Shin Ae rarely remembered having nightmares.

After breakfast, they go down to the river to wash their faces. They linger at the river's edge, sitting on the rocks. It would have been more sensible to set off in the cooler morning air, but none of them is really in a hurry, uncertain of what awaits them on the other side of the border.

Han Sa wants to know about Shin Ae and Jinju's hometown. They do their best to satisfy his curiosity but as they talk about home, Shin Ae begins to wonder what she'll tell her family. If she tells them the truth, they might turn her out, mourn her as dead. Perhaps it would be better if she didn't go back, if she just disappeared. She turns the questions back on Han Sa, hinting that perhaps she would rather stay in Seoul.

But before he can answer, she abruptly gets up and heads back to the tracks. She needs to walk, to move, to skip and twirl, to try to remember joy. Jong Nam is the first to go after her, following her lead. Soon after, Jinju and Han Sa join in, creating a game of follow the leader, each taking a turn until they wear themselves out and fall into a steady walk, Shin Ae quietly humming to herself.

Jinju spends the morning walk teaching Jong Nam Korean. They make up word games and try to learn about each other using simple language. Jong Nam is motivated and a quick learner. Jinju, on her part, seems to be a natural teacher. She toys with the notion that perhaps she could become a school teacher, but can't imagine how it would be possible. She hasn't even finished high school. She shakes her head to clear it of thoughts of the future, even if the future is only days or weeks ahead.

Shin Ae seems is content to walk along in her own little world, humming happily to herself. She isn't aware of Han Sa following her, listening to her sweet voice trailing in her wake. He is totally entranced by her. It must have started the first time he heard her sing. Her voice seeped into his being and he found it painful to imagine not being able to hear her sing again.

But it wasn't just her beautiful voice. He was intrigued by her ability to shake off her intense grief with her childlike ways, with her lack of self-consciousness. He felt a deep longing to be by her side, to protect her, to play with her, to be surprised by her. Like now as he almost falls over her where she's squatting down to look at two flowers growing between the tracks.

"Aren't they beautiful," she smiles up at him. For some reason, he feels like his heart is breaking. He squats down next to her to get a closer look. "Life must be very precious," he says. "If not, would trees grow out of rocks or flowers in railroad tracks?"

She's not so sure, having seen several of the women at the camps take their own lives. Not knowing how to reply she just smiles weakly and shrugs. He goes to pick one of the flowers to put in her hair, but she stops him, and he laughs at his own inconsistency.

They continue walking, though now side-by-side. Han Sa is wrapped up in his thoughts of taking her hand in his and barely hears her asking him a question. She's asking him about Seoul again. And again he feels his heart breaking as he grasps her fear of going back to her family, going back to a world that likely has no place for her. As best he can he describes the neighborhoods and the people of his home town. As he does so, he tries to imagine her in each of the scenes; what she's wearing, who she's talking to, where she's going.

Listening to him, Shin Ae thinks how nice it would be to be a man, to be able to return to people happy to see you. Or at least to be able to travel or live alone without people making assumptions about your character, your purity as a woman.

Ahead of them, Jinju and Jong Nam have stopped for the mid-day meal. It's hot and they're tired of walking. Jong Nam surprises them with his new vocabulary and ability to converse. "You're here! Come eat with us. It's so hot, you should rest." Seeing their surprised delight, Jong Nam is very pleased with himself, so much so that he jumps up and starts to dance, throwing his arms in the air and dancing with each of his saviors in turn.

Everyone takes up the dance, Shin Ae accompanying them with a nonsense song she makes up to an old folk tune. When the song ends they fall to the ground panting and laughing like old friends, together again after a long time apart.

After all the excitement, they eat in relative quiet, each content to be together, to be free. Jinju notices the way Han Sa has begun to look at Shin Ae and smiles to herself in a moment where everything seems possible.

Both Han Sa and Jinju see the cloud pass over Shin Ae's face, but can't see the longing she feels for a home that no longer exists for her. The longing that fills every part of her before she lets it go and gives her friends the barest of smiles.

Unable to do anything else, Shin Ae lays down on her side, curls herself tightly into a ball and quietly sings herself to sleep. They others feel the heaviness in the air and not wanting to talk or think anymore, join her in taking an afternoon nap.

KORYO 12

Tae Moon is the first to get up, his thoughts still jumbled. He doesn't even know how to consider such a far-fetched idea—an ignorant slave selling books to scholars and nobles.

He sits outside the cave, soaking in the cool predawn air, watching the sky shift and change from green to red to blue. Without knowing how or why, he decides to trust, to trust the two men who have miraculously appeared by his side, to trust life.

The cool air feels good, feels real. The sky is just beginning to lighten with hints of red still showing through the trees. Tae Moon begins to walk up the side of the mountain, up his favorite trail, up. As he walks, he focuses on his surroundings, more birds have arrived, the morning concert is brilliantly cacophonous, bursting with the joy of living. Finally he reaches his destination, a climbing tree with a view of the town below.

He climbs onto the lowest limb, leans his back against the trunk and stretches his legs out on the branch. Looking out at the view he remembers what brought him to this place.

Pictures of his life make their way through his mind's

eye. Fleeting images of his parents before he was traded away. He was about the same age as Chang Mi when he left them. Or rather, when they ripped him out of his mother's arms. He remembers trying to be brave so she wouldn't worry about him. Really, he was so scared he could barely walk.

He hated the stables at first, but once he got used to the horses he felt lucky to be around them, to serve them, to establish a mutual respect. They were better to him than any of the people he served. And though he was happy to be away from his master, he missed the horses.

It wasn't until the sun was up and shining in his eyes, that he began the walk back. Only then did he let himself begin to imagine their future, far-fetched as it was.

Entering the cave he found Chang Mi stirring the porridge and Shin Seo folding up his bedding. Chang Mi smiled and called out to Shin Seo, but he seemed to be as immersed in his thoughts as Tae Moon had been since waking.

It was another quiet meal, the men absorbed in their imaginings and Chang Mi humming to herself as she ate. Tae Moon and Shin Seo wouldn't be able to talk until later as they weren't ready to discuss the book stall in front of Chang Mi and couldn't leave her alone. Instead, after cleaning up, they practice their lessons, reciting and writing, and trying to make sense of the words' true meaning.

As they work, the smell of rain hitting the dirt permeates the cave, a gentle, steady rain. The kind that makes you feel safe and warm and happy to be working at home. The kind that leaves the world fresh and the sky clear blue when it's over.

When the rain stopped, Chang Mi got antsy and convinced Shin Seo and her father to play with her. She brought out her special stash of stones and they began to play. They marveled at how much better she was at it than them. But they tried their best, even making little bets when they took their turns. The loser had to serve the mid-day snack of rice and deer jerky.

After, the men went back to practicing their lessons hoping to gain the skill and confidence that would be required of them if they were to agree to Han Jin's idea. Chang Mi, on the other hand, picked up the fine brush he had given her, and began to draw the men at work.

Han Jin arrived as noiselessly as he could manage hoping to catch them at their studies. Standing at the entrance, watching his pupils absorbed in their task, he could easily imagine them working in the market. He just didn't know how long it would take to prepare them.

Shin Seo was the first to notice Han Jin as he looked up from his writing. Chang Mi quickly noticed the broad smile on Shin Seo's face and was up and running to her teacher before her father could even look up.

This is what family feels like, the yangban thought as his most talented pupil wrapped herself around his legs. Laughter came spilling out as tears welled up in his eyes. This is what love feels like, he thinks, as he smooths her hair and crouches down to take in her beaming face.

Chang Mi takes his hand and brings him to the table where the men have stood up in greeting. She sits and pulls him down to sit next to her. He notices how well her drawing captures Shin Seo and her father's concentration as they work at writing the characters accurately. It was impossible not to be amazed at her talent. What a waste it would be for her to remain a slave.

He checked Tae Moon and Shin Seo's work and was impressed. His whole life he had been told that education was only for the elite, that it was a waste for the common people to learn, that they wouldn't be able to understand anyway. It never made sense to him though—how could knowledge be a waste? Did Confucian thought really teach that only a select few could study the tenets? If so, he really couldn't understand how its ideals could be reached.

Chang Mi got impatient and asked if he had brought them anything. Her father, embarrassed, chides her for her rudeness, but Han Jin just laughs and pulls out some treats from his jacket and hands them around. The rice cakes are quickly devoured in happy silence, the sweetness lingering on their tongues and smiling lips. Almost in unison they each take a deep breath and thank their benefactor.

Finally, the evening's lesson begins. Han Jin can feel the new resolve in Chang Mi's father and understands that he has taken the idea of running a book stall seriously. Somehow, he is going to have to buy the runaway slaves new identities without making his servant suspicious. Once that is done, he can find them a place to live. It's only a matter of months before the cold will return.

"I'm hungry." Chang Mi's whine ended the lesson,

giving her father an opportunity to go out with Han Jin to get fresh water, and perhaps some fresh meat. But before getting up, Han Jin pulls a steamed bun out of his jacket to tide her over until dinner.

Tae Moon was the first to spot the soldiers and quickly hid, his heart pounding in his ears. Han Jin was surprised, but quickly regained his composure. They were from his father's friend's household; a man notoriously brutal to anyone of lower rank. One of the soldiers recognized him and came over to ask if he'd seen the slave they were searching for. He could imagine the poor slave being rolled up in a straw mat and beaten if he were found, and shivered slightly. Han Jin was grateful he hadn't seen the slave, hoping he would succeed in his escape. To protect his friend, he said he'd heard someone running in the other direction and sent them off looking.

Quickly, wordlessly, Han Jin and Tae Moon returned to the cave—getting water had just been a pretext for them to be able to talk away from Chang Mi.

When they arrive, their bleak mood was hard to miss, as was the lack of water. Even Chang Mi's bright smile disappeared in the face of her father's obvious anxiety. They all understood the need on this night to be quiet and alert.

The meal was bittersweet—they're grateful to be together, but all too aware of the gravity of their situation. When it was over, Chang Mi's father quickly convinced her it was time to go to bed. Chang Mi, acutely aware of the tension in the room, complied though she wanted to spend more time with them.

Chang Mi and her father prepare their beds and Chang Mi gets under the blanket. Her father strokes her hair and pats her chest to comfort her, quietly singing a lullaby until he is sure she's sleeping.

Finally, the men can talk freely. They all see clearly the need for Chang Mi and her father to shed their slave past with new identities. "Wouldn't it be possible to add them to my family register," Shin Seo wonders aloud. Tae Moon looks at him, barely containing his tears, then looks back at Han Jin hopefully.

"Interesting," Han Jin muses. "I'll look into it. For the right price, I don't see why it wouldn't be possible."

Shin Seo and Tae Moon look at each other at the mention of money. Shin Seo has little of it and Tae Moon none. Their debt to Han Jin is growing by the day and they can't fathom how they will ever be able to repay him. Han Jin read their thoughts, "First, I'm the one indebted to you. Before meeting you, life had little meaning or purpose. Second, you can pay me back when the bookstall is successful."

They talked a little longer before sending Han Jin off. Shin Seo wanted to walk with him, but only went as far as the tree outside the cave. He didn't dare leave Chang Mi and her father alone with the slave hunters out. Shin Seo remembered the young orphan and wondered if he was OK. Suddenly, feeling very tired, he bids his friend good night.

Once Han Jin disappears from sight, Shin Seo drops down on his haunches, resting his forehead on his knees, hoping the sounds of the night will drown out his thoughts.

Tae Moon sat awhile longer staring into the dying embers. Imagining a life where he was truly free—where no one could buy or sell him at their whim, where he didn't have to run away to protect his family—is nearly impossible.

He was being reborn, reinvented in this cave like a caterpillar in a chrysalis.

In a way, he felt grateful to his former master. Had his master not been such a rabid dog, he would never have left, would never have known that with a little courage, he could learn to have a dream, could see his daughter grow up free.

With these thoughts his strength came back to him, the fear abated and he was ready to lie down next to his amazing daughter. He was ready to dream with her.

MANCHURIA 5

Han Sa's heart is pounding with the whelm of emotion he feels watching Shin Ae lying asleep on her back, arms outstretched. He hasn't seen her look so relaxed, so at peace. Her eyes slowly open, then close again as she stretches herself awake. "Good dream?" he asks.

"Mmmm." She rolls onto her side, keeping her eyes closed to better remember the dream, the feel of it. "I was floating in a river, naked, at night. I was a man. There was a sound. Bees. Bees buzzing. But no bees were in sight. The water was cool and comforting." She spoke slowly, savoring each word, trying to hold on to the feeling.

Taking a deep breath, she opens her eyes and smiles, looking deep into Han Sa's eyes. A recognition passes between them that neither quite understands; they just know that they are happy to be together in this moment, in this time of transition.

Jong Nam bounds over, dancing and singing a song his mother had taught him. Shin Ae, laughing, gets up and joins in. Jinju also sings along as she packs up their belongings. Like that, Jong Nam and Shin Ae lead the way skipping and holding hands while Jinju and Han Sa happily follow the traveling show.

Before long they run out of steam and slow to a walk. Jong Nam begins to ask Shin Ae questions about her life before the war in his broken Korean. Jinju and Han Sa listen, each ready to step in. But Shin Ae calmly answers his questions, telling him in simple language of her family, of her many older brothers and sisters—their likes and dislikes, their talents and foibles, the ones she gets along with, the ones who scold her. She paints a picture of each, one by one. Jong Nam doesn't understand most of the words, but he listens carefully, trying to picture them as she does.

Jong Nam runs out of questions and gets lost in his imaginings of life in Korea. Growing up in Japan, he's only ever heard how primitive it is, how barbaric the Koreans are. But he's never quite believed it—his mother is the sweetest, most gentle person he knows; his father the coldest.

Shin Ae wanders off into the trees for some privacy. As she squats down to relieve herself, she feels an excruciating pain in her back where it had met with the barrel of a rifle when she tried to escape. She stifles a cry, but the tears can't be stopped. Arms wrapped around her shins, her head buried in her knees, she gives in to the flood of anguish; let's it wash over her. And just like the storm cloud that it is, it passes, the light filters in again, the tears end. She wipes her face on her sleeve, gets up, and runs back to her friends before they come looking for her; runs to Jinju, grabs her from behind and hugs her; lays her cheek on Jinju's back and holds her friend hoping Jinju knows just how grateful she is to her.

Jinju quickly gets over the surprise, slowly turns to her friend careful not to break her embrace, strokes the hair out of Shin Ae's face and gently holding her sweet friends face in her hands, lightly kisses her—once on each eye, once on the forehead—before gently pressing Shin Ae's cheek to her breast. If it hadn't been for Shin Ae, if Jinju hadn't had someone to take care of, she's sure she wouldn't have survived these last years, sure that like so many others, she would have taken her own life or succumbed to death in some other way.

Shin Ae pulls away taking Jinju's hand and together, hand-in-hand, they set off, skipping, behind Han Sa and Jong Nam who, somewhat embarrassed, had already started walking. Catching up, the women just crash into them and they all stumble, tumble with Shin Ae landing on top of a very surprised Han Sa.

A jolt of electricity passes between them as their eyes meet and Shin Ae quickly rolls off and gets to her feet. She's hit with a complex of emotions from excitement to panic—her heart pounding from elation and terror in equal measure. She runs, as fast as she can, trying to outrun the play of feelings coursing though her. The others follow, calling out for her to stop, but she can only hear the pounding of her heart, the sound of her breath until, breathless, she reaches a clearing and collapses, panting.

Jinju catches up with her, sits down beside her. Having felt the electricity that passed between Shin Ae and Han Sa, she too is caught up in her own thoughts and emotions. Jinju thinks of the boy her parents had wanted her to marry before the war tore them all apart. Where is that boy now, she wonders. Would his family still let him marry me?

She lets out a sigh and helps Shin Ae up so they can continue on their journey whatever their future has in store for them.

After walking along quietly for awhile longer it's time to stop for the day—the women's feet ache and they're all tired and the sun is low in the sky.

Jinju lays out the table while Han Sa and Jong Nam set off for firewood and perhaps a rabbit to roast. Shin Ae wanders off to see what roots or herbs she might find. Mostly, she just wants to enjoy the feeling of walking alone with no eyes on her, no fences, no fear of getting caught.

Shin Ae, Han Sa, and Jong Nam all return at the same time. Jong Nam builds the fire, Jinju prepares the rabbit for stew, leaving Shin Ae and Han Sa to go to the river to fetch water. Han Sa insists he can go alone and Shin Ae feigns being busy, but the others insist they go together. Their shy romance has not escaped anyone's notice.

They walk side-by-side, embarrassed, excited, too shy now to speak. Perhaps it wouldn't be so awkward if it were a romance that could extend beyond their journey home. But both know there is little possibility of Han Sa's family ever accepting Shin Ae, regardless of her recent past.

Even so, it's a relief for Shin Ae to know that she is still capable of falling in love.

On the way back, Han Sa tries to restore the ease they had shared by telling jokes. Even he knows they're pretty bad, but Shin Ae happily groans at each one and laughs in spite of herself.

It's a beautiful clear evening with a mild breeze gently caressing their faces. The horizon is painted in blazes of yellow, orange, and red all giving way to the deep cyan that comes as night falls. The crackling of the fire accompanies the emerging stars.

Just as the last bit of light fades, Shin Ae begins to softly sing a song her mother used to sing to her—a song each of their mothers has sung to them. And then they are all singing, all remembering. And when the song ends the sounds of the night takes over; crickets and owls, the buzzing of insects, and the quiet snoring of humans.

KORYO 13

Chang Mi awoke, her head fuzzy with camp fires and beautiful singing. She rolled over, melting into her father's back, holding his waist. She breathed in his warmth, his love. Her father rolled over to face her, to stroke her hair. To avoid the tears about to come, he began to tickle her and she to scream with laughter and delight.

At the sound of her scream, Shin Seo bolted upright. The look on his face only brought more laughter from the father and daughter making Shin Seo angry. Without a word, he stomped out of the cave, feeling as though he would suffocate if he stayed. Chang Mi and Tae Moon were surprised. They'd never seen Shin Seo get angry before, but each in their own way, understood his feelings.

Shin Seo's feet took him toward the river. He too was surprised at his anger, at his fear. He stopped and dropped down on his haunches tightly wrapping his arms around his shins and lowering his forehead onto his knees; tightly reigning himself in. He wanted to yell, to beat someone with his fists, to kick out and feel the resistance, to externalize the pain and rage. Instead he holds himself as tight as he can, presses his eyes into his knees and begins to rock himself, to rock until he can no longer contain his feelings and begins quietly to sob.

When the tears pass, he straightens himself up and takes a deep breath, savoring the cool morning air; lets the birdsong take over his thoughts. He notices the rays of light filtering through the trees and lets hope emerge from a place deep within.

He feels lighter than he has for awhile as he continues on his way to the water. When he gets to the stream bed, he takes off his shoes to feel the smooth stones under his feet as he walks. Stopping, he picks up a few flat stones and sends them off, watching them skip along the surface of the water before either sinking or making it to the other side. The skipping stones mirror how he feels in a way that he can't quite put into words.

As he looks down at the stones again, one stands out. He smiles and picks it up for Chang Mi imagining her look as he gives it to her. He carefully stows the small treasure in his jacket. In doing so, he finds the stone she had given him.

As he lightly holds it and rubes his thumb over it, he notices the smooth calm of it, remembers her handing it to him; remembers that moment when he still didn't know who she was to him. He nestles it next to the stone he found for her before washing his face in the cold mountain stream.

After drinking the clear clean water from his cold hands he's ready to go back to the cave. On his way he spots a rabbit and just as he's about to wield his slingshot, he decides to give it a reprieve. He's relieved that Chang

Mi had seemed to forget her desire to learn how to use one.
Chang Mi and Tae Moon were waiting for him. The
morning air had begun to warm so they decided to bring
the breakfast table outside. It was a beautiful morning re-
plete with blue sky, full sweet-scented trees, and birdsong.

Once the table was filled and they'd sat themselves
around it, Shin Seo told Chang Mi to put out her hand
and close her eyes. He pulled out the stone and placed
it in her little palm. "Whaah!" She traced the edge with
her finger, amazed at it's perfect heart shape. She stood
up, went over to Shin Seo and gave him a big hug from
behind. Shin Seo covered her hands in his, closing his
eyes, and drinking in her love.

After breakfast he decided to go into town. It had
been a few days and he was feeling restless. Chang Mi was
upset at being left behind but let it go since he'd brought
her such a beautiful gift. He urged her to work on her
writing while he was gone and to make a drawing for him.
She started to follow him a ways down the path, but her
father quickly grabbed her by the hand, the memory of
the slave hunters fresh in his mind.

Shin Seo's heart quickens as he nears the market. The
smells and sounds drawing him in. He walks slowly down
the market street, carefully looking at his surroundings
as if reading a book, a picture book, which would instruct
him on the secrets of becoming a book seller. Noticing
which stalls have a steady stream of customers and which
don't, he tries to understand the difference between them;
not just the book sellers, but all the merchants.

When he passes by the tavern where he first met Han
Jin he decides to stop in, hoping to find his friend. Han
Jin isn't there. Disappointed, he sits down anyway and
orders soft tofu stew.

Fully absorbed in his thoughts and his meal, he
doesn't notice that someone has sat down across from
him until he sees a spoon reaching into his stew.

Shin Seo and Han Jin can barely keep themselves
from laughing out loud in their delight at finding each
other. They remain quiet, cautious, agreeing to meet at the
warehouse before Han Jin reluctantly leaves his friend.
For the rest of the meal, Shin Seo's mind is racing, filled
with all the things he's noticed and the questions he has
for Han Jin. He finishes quickly and makes his way to
the warehouse.

Han Jin is already there, attempting to read as a distraction while waiting. It feels as though they haven't seen
each other for a very long time though it's only been a day.
Perhaps they're so happy because they found each other
without planning it, drawn to each other like magnets.

Shin Seo sits in front of Han Jin spilling out everything he's noticed, all his thoughts and questions before
Han Jin can say a word. Faced with such an onslaught,
Han Jin bursts into laughter. At first Shin Seo is confused,
then quickly joins his friend in laughing at himself. And
when they can't laugh any more, they just look at each
other, smiling, astonishingly happy to be together.

They spend some time talking about the market and
how to run a book stall before Shin Seo begins to talk
about his youth and his family and what led him to leave

his home. Han Jin listens, imagining as best he can the scenes of Shin Seo's life, his family members disappearing one by one until only Shin Seo is left.

"I envy you." Shin Seo is surprised at Han Jin's words. "You had a real family. Your mother and father were proud of you. You had both feet in your world," Han Jin explains. Shin Seo nods but says nothing in reply. He hears the truth in Han Jin's words, but still can't acknowledge that his life might have somehow been better than Han Jin's.

"It seems we always want what someone else has in this world," Shin Seo finally muses. "Why is it so difficult to be content with what we have?"

"Perhaps that's what true freedom is," Han Jin hearing the truth of the words as they come unexpectedly from his lips.

They sit silently for a bit, each man trying to see his life through the other's eyes. And then, all too soon, it's time to part ways again.

Han Jin couldn't go back to the cave with Shin Seo as he had family obligations, so they arrange to meet again the next morning. Before leaving the warehouse, Han Jin gives Shin Seo a present for Chang Mi in a small bamboo container.

Walking back Shin Seo notices the clouds just beginning to gather in the evening sky, their beauty in motion. He has no idea what the future will be like, but in this moment, he is truly happy to be living a life in motion, a life where each day is an adventure, stretching him in ways he had never imagined.

The disappointment on father and daughter's faces when Shin Seo arrives alone is unmistakable. Hoping to lighten their mood, he quickly gives Chang Mi Han Jin's present. She opens the box and her eyes widen. Shin Seo and Tae Moon crowd around her to see what it could be and find a small bottle of blue pigment inside. It seems Chang Mi has a patron hoping to nurture her talent.

She pulls Shin Seo down to sit next to her at the table where she has been doing her lessons. He's still amazed at how much quicker she is to learn the characters, to gracefully set them to paper. And she can read the Confucian tracts, even though their meaning is lost to her. Shin Seo and her father try to explain, as much to themselves as to her, but are unsure if they can really grasp the concepts themselves, still unsure if they have the right to enter the thoughts of scholars and nobles.

Now that Shin Seo has returned, Tae Moon leaves for a walk. He doesn't know how much longer he can take living cooped up, hiding in a cave, worrying about Chang Mi being found.

He takes a deep breath and smells the rain before he feels it on his skin. The cool drops feel like a gift as they gently beat down on his head, his shoulders, as they soak into his jacket, as they rain onto his face, his eyelashes, softening his vision. He lets go of the barrage of thoughts that filled his head all afternoon, the knots he can't quite unravel.

He climbs up to straddle his favorite tree branch, leans against the trunk, closes his eyes, and lets himself get lost in the sounds and smells surrounding him. Characters draw themselves in his inner vision, a parade of words, concepts fading in and out, dancing to a song of their own creation.

His eyes suddenly open as he hears a loud cheep and sees a goldfinch has landed on his perch. The bird, looking at him begins to sing. Tae Moon reaches out his finger and the bird hops up onto it continuing its song. Lifting the bird up so that they're eye to eye, Tae Moon whistles his reply. And then, with another cheep the goldfinch flies away, leaving Tae Moon with the message that life is a gift to be treasured.

Tae Moon is still whistling the bird's song when he returns to the cave. Chang Mi looks up from her dinner preparations, Shin Seo from practicing his writing, both puzzled. But it's not until they finish their meal and Chang Mi is lying in her bed that he tells them of his encounter with the bird; a perfect bedtime story to bring forth sweet dreams.

MANCHURIA 6

Han Sa hears the birds but can't quite tell where the sound is coming from. It seemed to be a single bird calling to him, but then turned into the cacophony of birds announcing the morning. He rubs his eyes open as he sits up, uneasy, not quite sure where he is. When he sees Shin Ae his heart unclenches and he smiles unconsciously. He can barely contain what he feels as he watches her sleep; can barely keep himself from walking over to her and taking her into his arms, from kissing her, stroking her cheek, her neck.

Instead, he lights the fire for the morning meal, meager as it is.

Jong Nam joins him, happy to have a *hyung*, an older brother. Han Sa begins to feel a bit morose knowing that he can't take Shin Ae home with him, that being with her would mean breaking from his family. Jong Nam senses his mood and screws up his face, acts like a clown trying to make Han Sa laugh. Finally, Han Sa acknowledges his new little brother with a smile and ruffles his hair. Han Sa knows that Jong Nam will follow him home, though neither has spoken of it. Since he's a boy it's not likely to present much of a problem. His brow knits again when he tries to imagine what will happen to Shin Ae.

"What's wrong with your face?"

Han Sa looks up to see Shin Ae hovering over him laughing. "Nothing," his worries melting into a smile. "*Noona!*" Jong Nam yells and delightedly wraps his arms around his new big sister almost knocking her over. Han Sa looks on with envy, wishing he could do the same.

Just then Jinju walks over and puts some millet on the fire to make into porridge. While the porridge cooks Jong Nam and Han Sa fetch more water so they can wash themselves and have some water for the morning journey. Han Sa walks there and back with a knot in his stomach as he continues to think about Shin Ae. It's not until they return and he sees the women laughing that he let's it go.

The air is crisp and cool for their morning journey. The pleasant weather helps them all feel light on their feet as they journey south alongside the railroad tracks. They play little games like follow-the-leader or who-can-make-up-the-best-song.

When they're all hungry, they find a spot with a view of the river to have their mid-day meal.

Jinju encourages Shin Ae to go catch some fish and Jong Nam and Han Sa eagerly offer to go with her. Jinju can't help but laugh at them as she sends them all off grateful for some time to herself. She's enjoying this space in between; this time to let go of the past few years, to just be before having to mold herself once again to fit the expectations of those around her.

It seems as though she had been holding her breath from the time she walked into the camp until the day she walked out and suddenly she can breathe again.

Shin Ae teaches Jong Nam and Han Sa how to spear fish with a sharpened stick. Jong Nam catches on quickly, but Han Sa is just hopeless at it and gives them a good laugh as he loses his balance and falls in the water.

Jong Nam is so excited about his new skill that he runs back to show Jinju his haul, with Shin Ae and Han Sa keeping up as best they can.

Lunch is filled with laughter and the intimacy that comes with being thrown together neither here nor there, where you can be yourself in ways you'd never imagined.

They set off once again, their hearts light, their bellies full. Life is unexpectedly good. Perhaps it's the lack of expectation that allows joy and light to filter into their darkened inner landscapes.

"Noona, sing us a song!" Jong Nam voices what the others are thinking. "Alright," Shin Ae responds, "but only if you all join in with me." Jong Nam is worried he won't know the song until he hears the familiar tune of Arirang and happily joins in with them while thinking of his mother singing it as she cooked. Of course she never sang it when his father was around, but often sang it when it was just the two of them. He can't believe he's finally going to see the land she was always nostalgic for. He vows to himself to make a lot of money so she can come visit him, perhaps even come live with him.

Shin Ae's not sure why she chose to sing that song.

Perhaps feeling so light was unnerving. Perhaps she wanted to feel a longing for her homeland that she didn't quite feel just now. Whatever her intention, the mood had altered by the time they finished singing. Though they had sung it together, their unity had dissipated as each retreated into his own thoughts and feelings.

Jong Nam wanted to make them laugh again, but thought better of it, decided to let them be and skipped on ahead of them, stopping every now and then to let them catch up.

When the sun was low in the sky they united once again in their desire to rest their tired feet and eat a small dinner. They fell in a heap on the cloth Jinju laid out. At the thought of what they must look like, Shin Ae began to giggle, then to laugh out loud and before long they were all laughing. When the laughter subsided, they felt refreshed and ready to eat.

Jong Nam asked them what their favorite places in Korea were and they each took a turn telling him. Of course, he was the first to fall asleep, his head resting on Jinju's lap. They finished their stories and lay down to dream, first to daydream what their new lives will be like before drifting off to the dreams that come with sleep.

KORYO 14

Han Jin wakes from a sweet dream of laughter and dancing; a dream of going home. A dream that seems to have no beginning and no end. For a moment he's confused, not completely sure where he is, who he is, until the room finally comes into focus and his servant enters with fresh clothes to change into before the morning meal.

They've always been polite with each other and no more. They seem to neither like nor dislike each other. The servant performs his duties, no more and no less, and when Han Jin leaves the house, his servant generally stays behind.

Spooning his soup into his mouth, he thinks about his mother, pondering how little choice she's had in her life. If it had been her choice would she have come into this household? Did she actually care about power, privilege, and prestige? It seemed too cruel a question to ask her, but he likes to imagine that she would have married simply, would have chosen love over power. Did his father still have any affection for her, his concubine?

After his breakfast, he spends time studying to keep his father happy. As long as he studies, he can spend the rest of his time as he likes. He can't imagine what his father would do if he found out who he's been spending his time with, what he's been teaching them, and what he's planning.

Since he started teaching Shin Seo, Tae Moon, and Chang Mi, he actually enjoys studying. The words have new depth, the characters a beauty he'd never fully appreciated. He's still unnerved at the hypocrisy of the aristocracy; tries to imagine what life would be like if they were actually to put the tenets they espoused into practice.

Oddly, what comes to him is not the utopian vision he expects, but rather the understanding that he can only be responsible for his own thoughts and actions. He has no control over how others live their lives. With this realization, a great weight is lifted; it's not up to him to change anyone, to change his father. He only has to do his best and be his best and everything else will fall into place.

With these thoughts come a desire to visit his mother. He finds her in her room at her embroidery frame concentrating on her work. She doesn't notice him so he just stands in the doorway watching her skilled hands at work helping a butterfly to emerge. When she finally looks up she just smiles at him, as if she knew all along that he was there.

He sits down facing her, legs crossed. They talk about nothing in particular, what they have or don't have to say to one another doesn't matter. All that matters is the love between them and the mutual recognition of the tight rope walk each does every day in this house they call home. Just before he gets up to take his leave he reaches out and squeezes her hand. Very briefly she looks at him before pulling her hand away and returning to her work.

Once out of the house it's always easier to breathe. He finds his way to the market to buy more paper and some steamed buns and fresh meat. He lingers at his favorite book stall trying to distill its secrets, what makes it his favorite. After a pleasant conversation with the bookseller, he finally understands that it's the bookseller himself that draws him in and keeps him coming back.

What a good day, he thinks to himself. The sky is a deep blue with wisps of white floating by. Entering the forest he notices that the leaves have fully emerged on the trees and all the birds have returned from their winter homes. The quality of light, now filtered through the canopy of green, is hushed, subdued, as if entering a room with paper-covered windows after the bright sunlight of the garden.

For the first time in a very long time, he's happy within himself.

When he enters the cool of the cave, it's empty. A sense of panic begins to overtake him before he checks himself. Laying his parcels down on the table, he leaves and heads toward the river.

Sure enough he finds them sitting on the bank enjoying the warm sun and cool water. He takes his time. Hidden in the shade of the trees, he squats down and watches them, taking in their familiarity, filling up with the gratitude he feels at having found them. It's as if he'd spent his whole life looking for them and now, miraculously, they had all found each other.

Finally, he walks over to them. Chang Mi nearly

tackles him with her embrace. Laughing he lets himself fall while tickling her, reveling in her childish screeches of delight. For a moment he's forgotten the danger; they all have.

They travel back to the cave with Shin Seo in the lead and Han Jin at the back, the men on high alert with Chang Mi between them. Along the way Chang Mi points out the edible leaves and roots she learned from her mother and together they harvest them for the afternoon meal.

The cave smells delightfully like steamed buns. Chang Mi runs to the table, "Whaah, look!" She holds up the fresh meat and a look of embarrassment passes across her father's face. He takes it from her and tries to return it to its buyer. Han Jin waves him off, "I was hungry for meat and good friends to eat it with." Tae Moon simply grunts in reply and sets it back down on the table. Han Jin, deliberately ignoring Tae Moon's discomfort, distributes the buns and together they enjoy the simple treat while sitting at the mouth of the cave.

They all help prepare the meal before sitting down to enjoy it. Even though they're as comfortable as family with each other, the men find it hard to talk. They're each still trying to understand how their future will unfold, trying to see it, to feel it, to believe in the possibility.

Fortunately, Chang Mi takes the opportunity to chatter away, telling her 'uncle' all about the previous day and her morning adventure at the river. She tells the men about the morning's dream where she is riding a small horse across a vast plain and about the drawings she made. Strange as the dream sounds, all three men feel they've had a similar dream though none of them says anything.

After their meal, there's a new urgency to begin their lesson. They spend some time reviewing the previous lessons before taking on the next one.

古之欲明明德於天下者 先治其國
欲治其國者先齊其家
欲齊其家者先脩其身
欲脩其身者先正其心
欲正奇心者先誠其意
欲誠其意者先致其知
致知在格物

Those of antiquity who wished that all people throughout the empire would let their inborn luminous virtue shine forth put governing their states well first; wishing to govern their states well, they first established harmony in their households; wishing to establish harmony in their households, they first cultivated themselves; wishing to cultivate themselves, they first set their minds in the right; wishing to set their minds in the right, they first made their intentions true; wishing to make their intentions true, they first extended knowledge to the utmost; the extension of knowledge lies in the investigation of things.

They each their tongues at how they felt hearing these lofty words. As before, they memorize each line, learning the nuances of the individual characters, before learning how to form them. At last, practicing them over and over, with each stroke of the brush they begin to gain confidence.

Chang Mi finishes learning the lesson first and begins to draw. This time her subject is Han Jin, painting his silk vest, trousers, and embroidered edges in blue. She had a way of capturing motion that was unique. Han Jin debated with himself whether to show her painting to someone or if it was still too dangerous. Patience.

When Chang Mi fell asleep, her head in her father's lap they decided it must be time to end the evening lesson. Han Jin and Shin Seo packed everything away while Tae Moon carefully put Chang Mi to bed.

Now that they had a goal, the men were a bit awkward with each other. Once they were seated around the table again, Han Jin pulled out a flask of rice wine. The familiar drink helped them relax, freed their imaginations, and allowed their words to flow.

Han Jin told them about his walk through the market, his thoughts on the book stall they would run, assuming all went well. Shin Seo and Chang Mi's father chimed in as well. They had a few ideas and lots of questions. What became clear was that they would need to bring in someone who had experience to help them, at least in the beginning. But that was impossible until Chang Mi and her father had new identities.

That was where they fell silent.

Tae Moon breaks the silence by thanking Han Jin for everything and announcing he is going to bed.

Shin Seo walks out into the sweet-smelling night with Han Jin. The sky is cloudless, star-filled, Äïa gentle breeze playing what must be the sound of heaven through the trees. They walk together filled with the satisfaction of knowing beauty, of knowing each other, until the path splits, Han Jin heading back to town and Shin Seo to the river.

Shin Seo hummed a melody his mother used to sing while doing her chores. As he walked toward the river, he felt like an integral part of his surroundings, and, for the first time, that somehow he was necessary, that his life had a purpose even if he didn't understand it; just as the river serves life in ways it has no knowledge of.

Floating on the water, finding the patterns of the constellations, once again he hears the buzzing sound. This time it seems that he has floated out of his body and up to the stars. His perspective changes and now he can see the tree tops, see the river, see his naked body floating. This is what freedom feels like, he thinks. And with that thought, he is once again floating on the water, looking at the stars.

Somewhat disconcerted, he quickly gets out of the water and heads back to the cave where he falls asleep, trying to recapture the feeling of freedom he'd felt.

MONGOLIA 3

Mongke wakes before his family, even before his mother who is always the first to rise. It seems like there's a message in his dreams, but he can't understand what it is so he lets it go. He's more concerned with leaving the yurt before anyone else wakes up. He doesn't want to talk to anyone until he's had a chance to sort out his confusion.

The sun is just coming up as he, on his horse, walks out of the encampment. The field before him looks like pure gold and smells of wet dirt. He almost feels like he's dreaming again. As he slowly surveys the landscape around him his horse suddenly takes off at a gallop, nearly leaving him behind. Mongke tries to reign him in, but something has spooked him and it's not until they reach the edge of the wood that the horse stops and nonchalantly lowers his head to graze as if nothing has happened.

At first Mongke is angry, but then starts to laugh out loud and hug the horse's neck. His horse is truly his best friend, understands him as no one else can. Mongke caresses the horses neck as he turns him around to head back to the yurt. He sees now that he need not be embarrassed. All he needs to do is act as if nothing embarrassing has happened. After all, he did better than most of the other boys who were all older than him. And while he was still confused, he at least felt like he could face his father and brother without shame.

He entered the yurt and took his place around the circle accepting the breakfast his sister handed him.

"I was pleased to see you handle the bow so well yesterday. It seems you will soon be among us."

Mongke looked over at his father who did not look back at him. He was about to explode with pride at his father's words but said nothing and tried to hide his smile. At that his brother mussed Mongke's hair and pinched his side. Mongke pushed him away, half happy, half annoyed.

MANCHURIA 7

They all woke up at the same time each wishing they could fall back to sleep, each wishing they could avoid the day. They could feel the nearness of the border, how close they were to their new lives; the excitement mixed with dread. Even Jong Nam felt apprehensive. He knew that his reception in Korea would be very different from how these three treated him.

Each lay there absorbed in their own imaginings.

Shin Ae and Han Sa had woken up with their backs pressed up against one another's, a small quiet comfort. Neither wanted to move, to break the bond. Silently, without a word, each spoke their heart to the other. It wasn't until Han Sa felt the gentle shaking of Shin Ae's back, of her tears, that he turned to wrap his arm around her, to gently put his other arm under her head, to cradle her, to bury his face in her neck.

He had never felt so conflicted; stuck between an impossible love and being a filial son. Neither was foolish enough not to know which he would choose.

Shin Ae tried to keep her thoughts on this moment, on this miracle, this moment of bliss. It was then that she felt him sobbing. The terror of war finally let loose from his gut.

She turned to him, stroked his tears away, kissed his eyes, pressed his head to her chest and stroked his hair, pressed her lips to his head as her mother used to do to hers when she needed comforting. He curled himself into her, let himself be a small boy again in his mother's arms.

Jinju was careful not to disturb them when she rose. She went over to Jong Nam to get him up, signaling to him to keep quiet as she led him off to fetch water for the morning meal. Walking down towards the stream Jong Nam asked Jinju about her parents. What he was really asking was what kind of relationship her parents had.

She smiled as she thought about them, feeling very lucky. Unlike Shin Ae, she knew that even though it would be difficult for them, they would accept her back into the family. Her father was strict but loving both as father and husband. And her mother had no reason to contradict him. Her obedience came of respect and love. Her father worked in their small store selling books and writing supplies. His mother helped out in the hours she wasn't taking care of the household chores.

Jinju stopped talking about them when she noticed how sad Jong Nam looked, asking him why. His answer came in a flood of Japanese; a domineering father, a cowed mother. Finally, he smiled and in Korean he thanked her for telling him about her happy family.

When they returned, they saw that Shin Ae and Han Sa had started the fire and were laughing as they prepared the ingredients for the porridge. All the awkwardness from the last couple days was gone and there was an intimacy that was palpable between them now. Jinju wished she could leave them here, let them live out their days in love.

Jong Nam did not share her feelings. He was too young to understand. He didn't hesitate at all to join them near the fire, to break in to their circle, accidentally spilling some of the water on Han Sa as he filled the porridge pot. He had no clue that Shin Ae and Han Sa only had a few days left; a few days before they would have to say their final farewells to each other.

The four of them took their time preparing and eating the meal. They even took the time to teach Jong Nam a new song which, of course, got them all up and dancing. It was a chaotic and joyous scene. And then it was time to pack up and continue their journey south.

Throughout the morning the collective mood moved like a symphony, swelling and withdrawing, like the sea as the moon exerts it's forces, pushing and pulling. There was laughter and silence, singing both exuberant and somber.

They lingered over lunch as they had over breakfast and napped in a huddle like puppies.

KORYO 15

Shin Seo woke up feeling lost, as if all his anchors had been cut. He had an uneasy feeling in the pit of his stomach. For the first time since he'd left the land he felt like perhaps he had made a huge mistake. He felt like running away, like going back to his old life where even the unpredictable aspects of life were predictable.

I must be crazy, he thought as he bolted upright. I should have just been happy with what I had. What was I thinking? His heart was pounding so fast that all he could hear was the woosh woosh of his blood pulsing in his ears. He closed his eyes and pressed his hand to his chest trying to calm himself.

Chang Mi could feel something was wrong as she came out of her dream; a dream of being on a huge boat with lots of oddly-dressed people. She saw Shin Seo sitting up, one hand on his chest, the other cradling his knees, rocking like a little boy. She walked over to him slowly, as you would to a wounded animal. "What's wrong?" she asked as she squatted beside him.

Her voice came as a sweet surprise lifting him out of the darkness that had enveloped him. He turned his head to look into her face. As much as he loved Chang

Mi, in this moment he desperately missed his mother and wished she were alive, that she hadn't left him. Was it to find her again as this small child that he left his home and all that was familiar?

"Nothing's wrong," he said making an effort to believe the words. "I'm fine; everything's fine." He smiled as he squeezed her hand and stood up. "I just need to clear my head."

Once out in the fresh air he starts to feel better, calmer. The air is heavy like a rain cloud. A uniform gray moves within and around the forest trees. He thinks that perhaps he's still dreaming, but a drop of dew, to heavy for the leaf on which it was resting, suddenly splashes on his head convincing him that he is indeed awake. Shin Seo wipes the wet away and takes a moment to breathe in the scene.

Even the birds' songs sound lazy and distant. The mist is a welcome relief, mirroring his inability to see what will happen from one day to the next. He walks slowly, feeling his way along the path to the river with heightened senses to make up for his limited vision.

He can hear small creatures scurrying away at his approach. Except for a gray rabbit calmly resting, holding its ground even when it knows it's been spotted. Shin Seo squats down in front of it, curious to see what will happen. The rabbit simply looks up at him and even hops a little closer. Shin Seo slowly reaches out his hand and lets the rabbit sniff it before carefully petting the rabbit between its ears. He continues to pet the rabbit until, having had its fill, it hops back into the wood.

169

He arrives at the mist kissed river where he removes his clothes and walks slowly into the cold water, enjoying the shock as more and more of his flesh is enveloped. He has an urge to swim to the other shore, to challenge his limbs, to breathe with purpose. He cuts through the water, in it but not of it, his arms moving with steady precision, his legs rhythmically propelling him forward until he reaches the shallow waters of the opposite shore. His goal accomplished, he turns and swims back without taking a rest, but slowly now, taking his time.

He turns over to float on his back. The rain comes gently, tickling his belly. Eyes closed, he opens his mouth to catch the drops before turning over again and swimming back to shore.

Shivering and invigorated, he gets dressed and walks back, walking quickly now, his stomach reminding him its time for breakfast.

Back in the cave he squats by the fire and warms his hands. Chang Mi is stirring a pot of porridge; the table is set. Tae Moon is sitting between the table and the fire studying the primer, following the strokes with his finger, naming each stroke as he traces its path.

Unconsciously, Shin Seo pulls the stone Chang Mi gave him from his belt and begins to caress it with his thumb. Chang Mi notices and smiles to herself, silently overjoyed to see he still carries it with him, that perhaps it brings him some comfort. Just as unconsciously, he puts it away when Chang Mi begins to fill their bowls.

Over breakfast they decide to spend the day studying. Faced with the vastness of the challenge they've set for themselves, all they can do is take one step at a time and give it their best effort. The rest is out of their hands.

They spend the day with brush in hand practicing both what Han Jin has taught them and new characters from the primer, correcting and encouraging each other as best they can. Chang Mi goes back and forth between writing and drawing, her skill with the brush a marvel and inspiration to the men.

At one point, while watching her with a father's pride, Tae Moon wonders what will become of her. So much talent in a world that will likely refuse to notice.

They continue well into the afternoon, breaking only for a small meal. Finally, Shin Seo looks up to see his friend watching them with a far-away look on his face. Chang Mi is the first to reach him, to take his hand and pull him to the table, to show him what they've been doing all day.

Han Jin is overwhelmed, tongue-tied. He fights back the tears threatening to breach their dam and finds a way to smile, to greet them with all the joy being with them again brings forth. He teases Chang Mi who is obviously waiting for him to produce the steamed buns he always brings, acting as if he's brought nothing for them.

It doesn't take long for her pitiful look of disappointment to win him over and he pulls out the still-warm buns and hands them to her. She squeals in delight, happily passing them out so they can all enjoy them together. The soft chewy dough with its hidden treasure of pork never fails to delight her and her delight always makes the buns that much more delicious for the others.

When they finish their buns, Han Jin looks over their work, impressed with their progress and determination. "It seems you're ready for the next lesson," he happily informs them and begins to recite,

物格而后知至
知至而后意誠
意誠而后心正
心正而后身脩
身脩而后家齊
家齊而后國治
國治而后天下平

Only after things are investigated does knowledge become complete; knowledge being complete, intentions become true; intentions being true, the mind becomes set in the right; the mind being so set, the person becomes cultivated; the person being cultivated, harmony is established in the household; household harmony established, the state becomes well governed; the state being well governed, the empire becomes tranquil.

Reciting the lines over and over the words seem to be speaking directly to them, as if they hold the key to their future.

When they've memorized the lines Han Jin finally picks up a brush, fills it with ink, and slowly writes the characters. Shin Seo and Tae Moon stand behind him watching intently, following the strokes with their fingers in the air.

Chang Mi, has begun to prepare the evening meal, creating a song out of the words as she fills the pot with rice and water and whatever else is at hand.

Any regret Shin Seo had felt in the morning has disappeared over the course of the day. Whatever might happen to them, these moments, this moment is worth whatever hardship might come.

They all spontaneously began to sing the song Chang Mi had created as they practice their writing and only stop to clear the table when the meal is almost ready.

When they had finished their stew and cleaned up, Han Jin produced some sweet treats which seems a fitting end to their day as they chat about this and that and nothing in particular.

Shin Seo walked Han Jin out. The gray morning had turned into a starlit night, the air crisp and vibrant. Shin Seo dared to feel hopeful that their plan might actually work.

"I found a way to add Tae Moon and Chang Mi to your family register."

Shin Seo just stared at Han Jin feeling like his heart might burst if he moved at all. Facing his friend he took Han Jin's hands in his and tried unsuccessfully to make words come out of his mouth. Instead he embraced him. The two stood there, Shin Seo's head buried in Han Jin's chest, unable to stop the tears of joy and gratitude.

Han Jin just holds him eyes closed, resting his chin on Shin Seo's head, a faint smile on his lips. This is what home feels like, he thinks.

Finally, Shin Seo separates from his friend to discuss the details of how to officially make Chang Mi and her father his family. They agree to meet the next morning and part with their hearts overflowing.

When Tae Moon has finished sending Chang Mi into the land of dreams, Shin Seo tells him the news. Just a few more days and An Jin and Chang Mi will be one step closer to freedom. They'll be able to look for a place to live, they'll really be family.

Shin Seo stays behind while Chang Mi's father leaves the cave for the first time that day. Tae Moon looks up at the sky to offer his gratitude to whoever or whatever is watching over him just in time to see a shooting star race across the heavens, then three more in free fall together. He takes a deep breath, arms outstretched, filling his lungs with the fresh mountain air, then sets off to find his favorite tree.

He makes himself comfortable on the branch, closes his eyes, and just listens, letting all his thoughts drift away unnoticed. He listens to the sounds of the crickets and cicadas and other night creatures. He listens to the sound he hears that is neither from within nor without, a sound that lives with him, that is always there to comfort him when he remembers to listen, a sound that he has never known how to describe nor ever told anyone about.

By the time he returns to the cave Shin Seo is asleep, snoring lightly. Tae Moon curls up next to his daughter and joins her in her dream world.

MANCHURIA 7A

Jong Nam woke up excited and nervous. Looking around he sees he's the only one awake. He closed his eyes again and tried to imagine Korea, piecing together all the descriptions he'd heard from his mother and his companions. He had a strange sense of having been there before.

Not knowing what else to do, he found a stick and began to draw, tracing the outlines of the trees surrounding them in the dirt. He didn't notice that Shin Ae was looking over his shoulder until she squatted down next to him.

"Keep going," Shin Ae said as he tried to erase his work, "It's beautiful!" Jong Nam kept his head down, aware that he was blushing at her praise. Then Jinju and Han Sa could be heard, oohing and aahing. "Whaah! You never told us you were an artist!"

Jong Nam was embarrassed. He'd never shared his drawings with anyone.

Han Sa walks over to his rucksack, pulls out a pencil and leather-bound notebook, and hands them to Jong Nam. Jong Nam just looks up at him, unsure what Han Sa wants him to do with them.

"Draw something for me," Han Sa commands. Jong

Nam just stares at him for a moment, considering, then shyly looks over at Shin Ae and Jinju and begins to draw, stealing glances in their direction every now and again. Han Sa manages to keep himself from watching over Jong Nam's shoulder even though he's dying to see what Jong Nam is doing.

Finally, Jong Nam hands the notebook back to Han Sa who is so moved he has to hold back the tears. There's so much love emanating from the page—the love the two women share for each other and the love Jong Nam feels for them. The picture shows them quietly talking to each other with the trees and mountainscape surrounding them. There's even a small rabbit off to the side eying them as if it wants to join them.

Han Sa doesn't know how to thank Jong Nam. Instead he presses the picture to his chest and bows his head toward his new young brother.

The women want to see it too, but Jong Nam is too embarrassed. For some reason Han Sa is also hesitant to show them, using Jong Nam's reluctance as an excuse to keep it to himself, his own personal treasure. Oddly, the women relent, perhaps recognizing that they too might be embarrassed.

To end the awkward moment, Jong Nam turns into the clown that he so enjoys being, making up nonsense words to a simple tune he knows. The others waste no time before joining in. They take turns making up nonsense verses, having quickly learned the silly chorus, and dancing like the animals of the forest.

Having worn themselves out, they sit down together.

There is an unspoken consensus that they will stay where they are until morning, that there is no need to rush to the border; the border will still be there tomorrow.

They sit there, out of breath, smiling like fools. Happy. Anyone to come upon them would have no idea what they'd been through or the trials they were heading towards.

"Do you know the Korean alphabet?" Shin Ae asked Jong Nam out of the blue. He shook his head, his heart suddenly sinking. "It's easy," she said, "wanna learn?" Instantly, his mood brightens again. Shin Ae jumps up and finds two sturdy twigs, handing one to Jong Nam.

As he watches she slowly traces the letters in the dirt,

ㅈ ㅗ ㅇ ㄴ ㅏ ㅁ

She waits for him to copy each letter before continuing on to the next. When he has copied all the letters she traces

종남

into the dirt and patiently waits for him to copy the letters. When he finishes, he looks up at her expectantly.

She points to and sounds out each letter as she carefully watches his reaction.

J—O—NG N-A-M

He finishes for her and jumps up and down shouting his new name over and over before squatting down and practicing, squealing in delight.

Meanwhile, Han Sa is writing the alphabet in the notebook—first the vowels, then the consonants. When Jong Nam finally pauses, Han Sa shows him the sensible script, sounding out each of the letters for him before handing him the notebook and pencil for a second time.

Han Sa demonstrates how to write each letter, the order of the strokes, using his finger to write it in the air, as Jong Nam copies it down. The women, meanwhile, decide it's time to prepare what will likely be their last meal in Manchuria.

Since they want it to be a special meal, they head down to the river to catch some fish. It's a glorious day and the river beckons. Neither hesitates to remove her overclothes and wade into the cool water.

The sky is a brilliant blue. As they float on their backs, holding hands, they take turns describing the cloudscape slowly morphing from this into that, from trees into dragons. They each savor the moment, savor the bond between them—silently vowing to never let go.

When they've had their fill, they catch the fish they'd come for and head back. Han Sa and Jong Nam are surprised at their soggy state having barely noticed that they'd left. Shin Ae and Jinju just laugh at them and urge them to continue with the lesson while they prepare the meal.

Sitting together eating, the silence is palpable. The play of emotions reflecting the play of clouds in the early evening sky. They want to make promises, but they're promises that can't be kept and to say anything else is too heartbreaking, too real.

Han Sa offers to clean up after dinner and the women let him because Jong Nam has asked them to write down some songs so he can practice reading. Just as he had hoped, Shin Ae sang the lyrics slowly while Jinju wrote them down.

By the time they were done, Han Sa had finished cleaning up and they all sat around the fire singing the songs for Jong Nam who sang along as he read the words. After singing all the songs they each laid down on their backs looking up at the star-filled sky.

Their thoughts moved toward the coming day and they quietly voiced the hopes and fears they had for their futures until there was nothing left to be said and they drifted off to sleep.

EPILOGUE

There. I've shared some of my tapestry with you, the threads that surface here and there.

Were you hoping for more? I think I was too, but we only get to see what we need to see, like the dappled light through summer trees.

Were you there with me?

Have memories surfaced you never knew you had? Have you dreamt in languages you didn't know you knew? You are truly much more than you ever imagined.

Sweet dreams!

ACKNOWLEDGEMENTS

Thanks, thanks, and more thanks.

Writing this book was an unexpected gift from Spirit with many helping hands. I couldn't have written it without the Thursday Night Writers group as a whole, and Doug Munson in particular, and all the friends who encouraged me along the way.

I'd also like to thank Brian Eno (Music for Airports) and Arvo Pärt (Für Alina) for providing the background music for the writing of most of the book.

I thank my mother for telling me the story of the escape from Ukraine, and my grandmother and great-grandmother for living it.

And, last but not least, I thank *you* for taking the time to read my stories. I hope it was time well spent.

CPSIA information can be obtained
at www.ICGtesting.com
Printed in the USA
FFOW02n1719280618
47228123-50026FF